Here's what they're saying

An absolute beach **must-read**, filled with love, humor, beautiful friendships, and relatable characters that will keep you on the **edge of your seat** until the very last page.

— *Kylie Wisniewski*, MIDDLE SCHOOL STUDENT

"...Teenage **first love adventures,** set in the famous Jersey Shore, the epitome of what it means to "go down the shore". Anyone who has spent summers at the Shore will relate, and teens who have never been will live and love vicariously through the characters. Those who are older will easily be reminded of what we experienced in our youth during summers at the beach. The **characters will suck you in** until you'll want to know what happens next, where they will end up with and whom. **A perfect summer read."**

— *Barbara Susinno*, REVIEWER

Casey of Cranberry Cove is all about **first love**. All the nervousness, awkwardness, excitement, and heart break. Susan Kotch captured all of these elements as she takes us on this whirlwind ride with Casey. **I enjoyed every moment!**

— *Rebekah Triolo*, EDUCATOR

i

Casey is a young girl experiencing what it is like to have her **first summer love**. This book will **make you laugh** and sometimes it will **pull at your heartstrings** but you grow with the characters and learn with them. *Casey Of Cranberry Cove* is a **fantastic read** and I hope everyone finds comfort in the characters just as I have found myself.

— **Mayerly Benavides, High School Student**

Victoria,

May all of your beach days be sunny! ☺

Casey of Cranberry Cove

Susan Kotch

Susan Kotch

First Edition 2015

10 9 8 7 6 5 4 3 2 1

ISBN

13: 978-0692402603

10: 0692402608

Credits

Cover Design: Capooter

Hibernian Publishing, LLC

New Jersey

Dedication

To my husband and son for their support and encouragement.
To my brother who believed I could do anything and everything.
We lost you too soon.

To my 8th grade students who cheered me on, and to whom I challenge that everyone has a story within, and it is so important to get that story onto paper.

And to the seaside resort of Lavallette, NJ, which provided the inspiration and the perfect setting for my story, and gave me years of my own childhood memories, many of which found their way into this book and the lives of Casey, Phoebe, Nick, Jase and Zack.

Acknowledgements

This book would not have been possible without the help of some very fine people who found their way into my life. Thank you to the wonderful team of Mike and Gail at Hibernian Publishing who took a chance. Thank you for making my dream become a reality. A huge thank you to my students Mayerly, Briann, Kylie and Shealyn who cheered Casey on from the beginning, and who are definitely on #TeamJase. I thank you for pushing me forward. Thank you, Casey Morrison, for providing inspiration, to my son, Jase, who is a lifesaver to me, and my very pulled-together niece, Phoebe. I thought of her whenever her namesake ran across a piece of seaweed. Thank you to my teacher friends who support me daily in and out of school. And Barbara Susinno, you were a great first-round proofreader, and I will treasure my sweatshirt always.

I emerged from the surf with my hair clumped and strewn over my face, spitting a salt water stream from my mouth as snot ran from my nose. My bikini top had settled up under my chin. My bottoms were filled with sand and broken shells. Very attractive. The perils of a boogie boarder.

"Did you see that? Did you see that ride?" I spit as I screamed over to my friend Phoebe who was still floating out in the water. She wasn't able to catch that monster wave that just made me swallow half the surf and probably a jellyfish or two. "Phoebes! I am still the champion!" I saw her doing some odd hand movements over her neck and stomach which I couldn't quite decipher. It looked like she was having some type of seizure. Finally, after making my way out closer to her, I heard her.

"Pull down your bathing suit top, you doofus! Didn't you hear me yelling to you?"

Now I knew what she was doing.

"It's all the way up to your neck, Casey! Didn't you see people looking at you?" She continued to scream at me, half laughing, half scolding. I ducked under the water to readjust the suit and put the girls back into hiding. That's the problem with boogie boarding in a two-piece suit. It can get messy. But it was the first day of the summer season, and no one wears a one-piece at the beach until the desired base tan is achieved. Then, and only then, do you get down to business in a practical one-piece.

"Sorry." I tilted my head and dipped under the water to fix my hair which was still plastered to my face and neck. "Think anyone saw?"

"Oh, no, I'm sure all the men on the beach are looking for those elusive dolphins through their binoculars. Surely, they aren't looking at some crazy teen girl who decided to flash the entire beachfront. See? They are all on their cell phones now, probably telling their buddies to hurry up and get here to enjoy the warm breeze and to check out the crazy teenager with no top on." She looked at me with a stern face, but then it softened. "You really need to wear a one-piece when you do this," she smirked, but with concern.

"But I have to get a base tan."

"I know, sweetie, but some of these men are over forty, and I don't think their hearts, or their marriages, will be able to withstand you boogie boarding in front of them anymore. We're getting older, and I just think we need to grow up a bit here. Mentally, that is."

Ugh. I hated when Phoebe said that. She was always the more mature one out of us. I was the one who would pick up a dead fish from the beach and put it on her towel while she slept so she would wake up screaming at the sight of it. Also, I would dig for the sandcrabs with my hands. This way the weekly beach renters could see how the little critters dig back under the sand with their hind legs as the waves receded from the shore. Phoebe hated everything fishy, smelly or slimy, and I always attributed it to the fact that she didn't grow up here. She and her family owned a summer home and would come down once school ended in June. They would stay until the day before school started in September. That's how I met her. It was about six years ago, but I've been friends with her ever since. Summer friends. That's how things are around here. You have your summer friends, and your winter friends. You are inseparable from June until August, and then you don't speak to each other until the following summer. But somehow, you always seem to pick up right where you left off when you see each other again. Phoebe and I had very different personalities, but we quickly became the best summer friends.

I, on the other hand, grew up here. The winters are cold, damp and quiet. Very quiet. Many of the businesses in town close after the warm weather leaves, and then open again in spring. There just aren't enough people to sustain them during the off-season. But there are people who live here. We have a school (although very small), and a few restaurants that stay open. But we make our own fun all year round.

A beach resort town is a special place to grow up. Cranberry Cove is situated on a barrier island on the east side of New Jersey. It's about a quarter mile wide and thirteen miles long. It connects to the mainland by three bridges that are spread throughout. It's surrounded by water — the Atlantic Ocean to the east, and Barnegat Bay to the west. We get to enjoy the most spectacular sunrises and sunsets. It only has about 2,500 people that live here full time. In the summer months, it explodes to 25,000 people. They own or rent the homes and look forward to enjoying what the town and the island have to offer.

Cranberry Cove is great. Along the bayfront, there are tennis courts, crabbing and fishing docks, sandy beaches and playgrounds, and a gazebo with grass and trees. Concerts are held there and outdoor movies are shown on cool summer nights. The town's oceanfront is just twenty blocks of white sand beaches with a boardwalk to stroll. There are also benches so one can sit to count the stars at night. It's pure bliss, and it's the best place to live no matter what time of year it is.

Many of our summer visitors are from the northern part of the state. They rent the homes here for a week or two as their vacation. The great part about the Jersey Shore is that once you figure out what your favorite beach town is (and there are many!), you tend to rent the same house during the same weeks every year. That's how I met Phoebe. Her parents came down here for ages, and when Phoebe and her brother were born, they continued to vacation here. About six years ago, they decided that two weeks out of the year was not enough. They caught the bug. They wanted more. So they bought a house here. A small bungalow that was right on my block. The old owners retired to North Carolina, and put it up for sale on a Tuesday. By Wednesday, the "for sale" sign changed to "under contract" and the rest was history. I met Phoebe the day she moved in and we've been friends ever since.

As we continued to float on our boards awaiting the next big wave, we didn't speak. We fell into a kind of lull that is so typical of us. We often got lost in our thoughts. The background noises of kids laughing and splashing, combined with the cries of the seagulls and the crashing of the waves, was always very soothing. It's easy to drift into a trance. And that's where we were until I heard Phoebe let out a scream.

"Auuughhh!" The scream was accompanied by some crazy type of acrobatic movement as she ended up about ten feet away from me. "I think a fish swam up against me! Gross!"

"Calm down, it was just a piece of seaweed." I picked my leg up into the air and unwrapped a piece of kelp. "What is your problem, girlfriend?" I gave her my you-are-such-a-wimp look and threw the kelp at her. She stuck her tongue out at me, resumed her position on her board, and we continued on with our trance. I rested my head on my arm and glanced towards the shore as we continued to float and rise over the waves.

The view of the beach from the water is always spectacular. There is nothing that beats the first day of the summer season at the shore. Families begin to arrive with their wheelie carts filled with every shovel, pail, Tonka truck, and Frisbee they own, along with old bed comforters, brightly colored beach umbrellas and sand chairs in tow. The youngest kids are usually glistening with white pasty sunscreen and hats. The parents are huffing and puffing trying to map out the perfect territory — one that will allow them to keep their eyes on the kids in the water without being too close to the rising tides that will surely return throughout the course of the day.

The landscape began to change as the colorful umbrellas sprung open; my eyes continued to search until I spotted what I'd waited for all fall, winter and spring to see — Jase. Jase Pendleton. The hottest lifeguard this town had ever seen. Tall, lean, muscular, already tan, and wearing the telltale uniform of the lifeguard staff – red board shorts with a seagull emblem. Boy, did he look good. And, he was Phoebe's brother.

Yup. Summer had officially begun.

The sun was high in the sky. Phoebe and I decided to take a break from boogie boarding and get to work on that coveted base tan. The sooner I had it, the sooner I'd be able to get into the one-piece and show the world my killer boarding moves. Plus, I know Phoebe would rest easier knowing that I wouldn't be locked up for indecent exposure.

At our base camp — also known as our spot on the beach — Phoebe enjoyed lying out on a towel, but I preferred sitting up in my sand chair. Their low-to-the-ground profiles allowed your legs to stretch out, and the reclining back allowed you to get maximum UV ray damage. But I wasn't worried; I always sun screened. Besides, I certainly didn't want to get wrinkled before my time. Plus, I like to read on the beach. You just can't do that comfortably while lying on a towel. It's too awkward. The chair also afforded me the luxury to scope out and keep an eye on the lifeguard stand where Mr. Hottie was stationed. I liked to watch the steady stream of girls approach the stand in an attempt to get his attention. *Like the string bikinis they wore weren't going to do that anyway.*

Today's base camp position was perfect. The north breeze was carrying the sounds from the lifeguard stand towards us, so I was really able to hear everything the girls said to Jase and his partner-of-the-day, Jessica.

"Ummm, can you tell me what the water temperature is?" This one was wearing a blue and purple triangle over her butt which was accompanied by two smaller triangles over her chest, held together with what seemed to be, from this angle, dental floss. Her hand was over her forehead, shading her eyes from the sun, and she had positioned herself perfectly next to Jase's side of the chair so from his view, he saw everything she had to offer at this point in her life. She looked to be about seventeen, perfect white teeth, brown hair blowing gracefully in the breeze. She used one foot to brush sand off the other as she balanced in this position. I wanted to go over and offer her a napkin to wipe the drool off her chin.

"It's about sixty-eight degrees now," Jase answered authoritatively, as I know he takes this job very seriously. His gaze lingered at her a few seconds longer than I'd liked, but he quickly realized it and recovered, reverting his gaze back to the surf where it should be at all times. She hesitated.

"Thanks." She turned and skulked away, but not before stopping to bend over to attend to that imaginary bit of sand that she felt was still stuck to her foot. He never glanced over. I chuckled to myself. *These girls will stop at nothing.*

"Stop looking at my stupid brother and look at this cute sundress I found in this magazine." My fantasy, which I just got started on in my head, starring her brother, was quickly wiped away as I directed my stare at her and the stupid magazine she was so delicately shoving into my face.

"I'm not looking at him. I thought I saw a whale." I smirked, and squinted toward the water.

"No you didn't. You are looking at him."

"Well," I admitted with a bit of a blush that you really couldn't see because my base tan was now beginning to take shape, "have you noticed how really good looking he is this year? He has nice muscles and he looks taller. What happened to him over the winter?" I hadn't seen him around the neighborhood since Phoebe and her family arrived for summer, although I certainly had tried.

"No, I hadn't noticed his muscles, thank you very much. He's my brother, you doofus. No one looks at their brother that way. I have noticed some of his friends, though. They are looking pretty hot."

"Yeah, well, I'm telling you your brother is definitely hot. I haven't seen him since last year. He's — he's matured."

"Oh really!" Phoebe blurted out to me. "My brother? Mature? Honey, never use those two nouns in the same sentence!" She snickered into her magazine that sported a great photo of Leonardo DiCaprio on the cover with the words HOT HOT HOT across it.

"How old is he now?" I questioned, returning my glance in his direction as the next two lovelies approached his side of the stand.

"Just turned seventeen last month. Driving now. The only good thing is Mom makes him drop me at the mall and pick me up." She flipped over the page to reveal THE TOP 10 REASONS WHY YOU SHOULD EAT VEGETABLES. *Wow. Earth-shattering.* "Since when are you so interested in my brother?"

"Since he's HOT HOT HOT," I mimicked the magazine cover. I guess she never realized that I've always had a bit of a crush on her brother; he's about three years older than me and exactly my type, although I'm not sure what that exactly is yet. Phoebe picked her eyes up and looked at me and then burst out laughing.

"You're a doofus," she said warmly and with love to me, and then lowered her eyes to read about the vegetables. I smiled and looked back at the lifeguard stand, as the two latest victims skulked away in defeat; I was unable to distract my favorite hunky lifeguard from fulfilling his duties.

"Hello? Hello? Earth to Casey?" I felt my foot being kicked, the coolness of shade on my face. I opened my eyes to see Phoebe standing over my chair. "Wake up! I'm sweating and need to go in and I don't want to go alone."

"Afraid a shark might get you?" I asked with all seriousness. "They've been spotted by some fisherman. Did you hear the reports?"

"Why are you telling me that? Now I'm not going in!" Phoebe whined, stomping back to her blanket and pouting. She was deathly afraid of sharks, so of course, I would mention them just to make her crazy.

"I'm only kidding, you doofus." Hey, if she could call me one, I could do the same. Besides, we used it as a term of endearment. "Anyway, the sharks would go after the smaller kids before us. Tastier and easier to swallow." I gave her my most sincere and matter-of-fact look; she wrinkled her nose at me and probably cursed me under her breath. I may have missed that part. "Yes, I'll go in with you. C'mon." I pulled myself out of my sand chair with poise, as it takes some practice to get to a standing position.

We made our way down to the waterline, and I shot a glance up at the lifeguard stand as we passed. I just wanted another look. We made eye contact.

"Hey, Casey, how's it going?" *Huh? Me? He's talking to me?* I smiled and slowed my speed down just a fraction. I might have added a little bit of a hip wiggle, but I'm sure it wasn't too noticeable. "Phoebes, watch for the sharks!" He obviously had my sense of humor as far as busting on Phoebe goes.

"Hey, Jase, how are you?" I managed to say, and turned back to Phoebe in time to catch her sticking her tongue out at him. *What's wrong with me?* I've spoken to him a zillion times in the past, and never felt this way around him, but this year it's different. The realization hit me. I had developed a crush. This changed everything. I sighed to myself.

"You know Boob Girl?" I heard Jessica, the other lifeguard, say to Jase. I continued my trek down to the surf with Phoebe. Thankfully with my back to him, Jase couldn't see me blushing. Note to self: Time to wear the one-piece.

The water was chilly, but felt good since we had baked for an hour in the sun. We made our way gingerly over the small breakers, turning our backs to the waves. We jumped as we reached the point where they were rolling in and breaking on our thighs. Never sure why people did this, since it's inevitable that everyone at this point was going to be wet anyway. We held our arms up out of the water, like that was going to help. It didn't. I guess it was just a reaction to do that.

The next wave rolled in and I decided it was time to bite the bullet. I dove into the wave as it broke and I came up on the other side of it, hair slicked back. I adjusted the suit. No need to have the cops called at this point.

Phoebe still continued to dodge the waves, so I decided to help her get on with this swim. I headed over to her, wrapped my arms around her and brought her down into the next wave. We emerged and she spat water in my face.

"I wasn't ready!"

"Well, now you're in, so let's get on with it." Again, I got the tongue stuck out at me but a giggle accompanied it so I knew I was forgiven. I began my swim away from the shore and out to where the waves were forming. If boogie boarding was my thing, it didn't hold a candle to my skills as a body surfer. Get ready, forty-year-old-married-men. Raise the binoculars; here I go.

There are only a few brave souls who have ventured out today past the breakers. It's usually the spot where the old ladies in bathing caps will go to avoid the splashing and knocking around that occurs where the waves break and rumble to shore. Out here, it's a slow ride of lifting over the waves, floating in the sun, and exchanging gossip and small talk with other floaters.

But, this is also where the serious body surfers congregate. People of all ages, sex and skill level will gather here amongst the bathing cap ladies and await the first sign of the "big one" — that one wave that will ultimately bring you all the way to the shore. The one that will cause you to beach yourself like a dead whale, with belly scraped and bathing suit filled with sand and anything else that you ran over. It's the elusive wave — the one that only comes once in a while. And if you miss it, you are left to watch with sadness the lucky few. Not to mention, you have to hear about it ten minutes later as they recall for you every bit of technique they used, while adding the phrase "I can't believe you missed that one" into every other sentence.

Phoebe never made it out this far. She's got that shark thing going on, and the deeper water freaked her out. I took my place next to an old lady wearing a white bathing cap sprinkled with yellow and blue flowers and smiled at her. She looked content. I didn't think she'd be any competition for me. But as I sized up the others, I saw a guy with a determined look on his face. Yes, this guy was serious, and I was ready for battle. We gave each other a barely perceptible nod and somehow we knew it was "game on." Turning to look out to sea, we waited for the slightest sign that a wave was forming. One began to head towards us and we moved to get into position, but as it came nearer it was clear that it wouldn't have the power to take us in, so we both eased up and let it slip by us. The lady in the cap who was floating on her back, just floated over it with ease. She'd obviously been sizing up waves here for years.

The next wave, however, was huge. I saw it start to poke out of the horizon and got a shiver at its size. It had potential. I heard someone down the line yell "here it is!" and I positioned myself perfectly and began to swim with it, waiting to feel the lift of the wave and that sure sign that I'd caught it. With one last push of my arms, I was positioned perfectly to take this one directly into the shore. I glanced to my right. The competition was also on the move. He was trying to catch it as well. The wave grabbed me. I was floating on top. I survived as the wave broke, still with full forward momentum. I'd caught it. White water splashed all around me and I rode it towards the beach. *Uh, oh.* I saw an old man in front of me. He was a bit shaky on his legs. He was eyeing the wave and me in it. He didn't know which way to move. I headed right for him. *Commit, already, mister. Pick a side.* He did. He moved left. So did I. We collided. I surfaced. My bathing suit top was around my neck. Again. This time I noticed quickly and adjusted it. Then I reached down to help him up.

"Sorry." It was all I could muster.

"Hey, nice ride," he said. I smiled and turned to make my way back to Phoebe who was freaking out because she was being attacked by another piece of rogue kelp.

"Did you flash him?" Phoebe looked at me sympathetically as I finally reached her.

"Yes. But I think he was too busy pulling up his own suit to notice. Beside, he's like sixty-five. Not sure he even remembers what they are." I swam back out and positioned myself for the next wave as I heard Phoebe lovingly call me a doofus.

"I'm getting out! I'm freeeeezing!" I heard Phoebe yelling out to me from the spot where the waves were breaking right on her. After six perfect rides into the shore (all after my run-in with the old-timer and the bathing suit mishap), I was exhausted, so I nodded to my fellow body surfers and began to head in.

"Nice riding," my competition said to me with a nod of his head.

"You, too," I returned the compliment. We actually bonded when I found out that bathing cap lady and the old timer were husband and wife, and she complimented me on how gracefully I was able to take him out with my first ride in. She swam in after that to check on him, and I just turned to my competition and shrugged my shoulders in an "I'm sorry" sort of way.

I reached Phoebe and both of us floated and let the waves pull us into shore. When we were in knee deep water, I was able to really examine the red skin on my stomach from running up onto shore and through the tiny rocks and shells that lined the shoreline. I saw it as the battle scars of a successful round of body surfing. Phoebe just looked at me and called me a doofus. "Another reason why you need to wear the one-piece," she said. I just smiled. She just didn't have the same passion as I did about a successful round of riding the waves.

We headed back up to gather our things, ready to head home after a very productive first day on the beach. With the start of summer came our rite of summer passage — the summer job. We both landed a job for the second year in a row at the local ice cream shop — the Polar Palace. It's a great place to stay cool and check out the vacationing hotties that wander in each evening at the town's only bar/restaurant, The Crabby Tuna. The Tuna is packed every day for lunch and dinner, and most nights there's a band, so we got to rock out to the live tunes as we scooped and bagged. The money wasn't great, but it passed the time, and allowed us our romps at the local boardwalk on nights off. Phoebe loved working there. I tolerated it.

As I picked up my towel and shook the sand off of it, my eyes were suddenly cast into darkness as a pair of hands covered them, and a hoarse "Guess who?" followed. A shiver ran through me. I knew that voice. It was a constant in my ear all last year, a third wheel to Phoebe and me as we played through our July and August. Our other bestie, Nick Alexander, had finally arrived in town.

"Nick! Where have you been? I missed you!" I yelled, and spun around to see a very much taller and more handsome Nick, standing in front of me. He was smiling his 1000 megawatt smile. Phoebe had already jumped onto his back and wrapped her hand around his neck like she was riding a bull. Nick was our rock, the go-to guy who hung out with us every day and night. He put up with our silliness and PMS. He lived in North Jersey now, but lived here all year round in Cranberry Cove up until a couple of years ago when his parents divorced. His mom moved back north to be with her family and took Nick with her, but his dad stayed here in town where he grew up. Nick now spent summers at the shore with his dad. I got to see him a few times during the off-season for holidays or visits. It was as if he was still a local.

"Hey, Babes! I've been looking for you! Just got down today and had to find you before I even unpacked. You guys leaving already?"

"We have to work tonight. We go in at six. But we'll be out at ten. Wanna hang out afterwards?" Phoebe was all over this one. I always thought she had a thing for Nick, but when I questioned it, she denied it.

Nick was beaming. "Sure. I'll unpack and then head up and hang out until you guys get off. We're doing a barbecue tonight, but I should get up there by around nine. Got a little surprise for you." He turned to me. "How's the waves?"

"Great! I only flashed once today."

"Twice," Phoebe reminded me. "And she only ran one old guy over."

"Nice belly burn," Nick said as he looked at my stomach. "I think you need a one-piece." I just smiled. *Everyone's a critic.*

The Polar Palace sat in the center of town, nestled between The Crabby Tuna and Benny's, the local pizza joint. All of the businesses do well in the summer as scores of tourists walk the sidewalks enjoying the fresh salty breezes and beautiful sunsets.

They paid for a week of bliss and they plan on enjoying every minute of it. The shops in town offer touristy trinkets, clothing, beach essentials, gifts and boxes upon boxes of salt water taffy; the perfect item to bring home to the neighbors. They are stuck back up in North Jersey watching your dog while you spend time at the beach.

Besides walking, the second most popular mode of transportation in town is the bike. Beach bikes are the bike of choice, which allow for cruising the streets without the hassle of hand brakes or gear shifting. You sit up straight, and simply pedal backward to stop. No hassle. The beach bikes of choice for the locals are the old rusty ones. The summer residents and tourists prefer the new sherbet-colored ones. You'll see them all over town parked in bike racks at the beach and in front of the stores.

Cranberry Cove is like a fairy-tale town. No one locks their bikes or their homes. It's as if everyone thinks that because they are on vacation nothing will happen. Usually it doesn't. Sometimes it does.

Text between Casey and Phoebe:

Casey: u ready to go?
Phoebe: yes. what r u wearing?
Casey: clothes
Phoebe: duh. what kind?
Casey: ?
Phoebe: last year's Polar Palace shirt? duh!
Casey: yes
Phoebe: I don't have mine
Casey: Just wear any shirt!
Phoebe: what color?
Casey: ur a doofus.
Phoebe: takes one to know one
Casey: I'm leaving now. Get your butt outside.

I jumped onto my rusted out beach bike, and headed four houses up the street to Phoebe's bungalow to pick her up. Just as I arrived, Jase was walking up the driveway, heading home from his lifeguard shift.

"Nice rides today, Beach Girl. I saw you wipe out that old man."

I blushed. "Well, he didn't commit soon enough to which way he was going to move. I took a chance and was wrong. It happens."

"You had a few other nice rides though. I was watching."

"You were?" *Darn, that sounded too anxious!* I looked down. "I really scraped up my stomach."

"You need to wear a one-piece." He smirked, turned and headed to the front porch. His hand on the door handle, he looked back. "See ya tomorrow." And with that, he pulled open the door and disappeared inside.

Phoebe came out seconds later wearing a purple flowered shirt that looked too pretty to be wearing while slinging ice cream. She must have seen the look on my face and read my mind. "It's only until they give us this year's Polar Palace shirt," she said.

I nodded, and she hopped on her sherbet-colored beach bike and off we went.

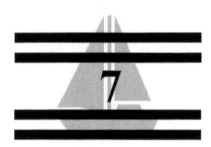

The Polar Palace isn't a palace at all, but a rundown yet cozy nook of an ice cream parlor. It is decorated with wooden replicas of beach badges from all the neighboring beaches on the island. Beach badges are a Jersey thing — you need to buy one and wear it or they don't let you on the beach. The rest of the United States seemed to have this thing called "free beaches" going on, but here in Jersey, you paid. Not that anyone really minded here at the Cove. The beaches were kept really clean, and people liked noticing everyone else's badge. People seemed to wear them like a badge of honor.

Phoebes and I parked our bikes outside at the bike rack. It was already crowded but we found ourselves a spot. Phoebe pulled out her bike lock and locked up her sherbet-colored beauty, but my rusty old hunk of steel just sat freely. Believe me; no one was going to take mine with the smorgasbord of pretty colored Schwinn Cruisers that were out here tonight.

The jingle of the door bells alerted the workers and the guests of our arrival. The few seats that were in the Palace were full. The music blasting from the restaurant next door was hardly recognizable over the laughing and talking of the patrons. Everyone seemed to be having a great time tonight at the Polar Palace.

Phoebes and I made our way through the maze of toddlers who seemed to have set up a camp — of some sort — in the middle of the floor. We slipped behind the counter to the stockroom to find our new Polar Palace shirts, which happened to be sporting a fuchsia pink color this year. I think they looked hideous and I let Phoebe know so. She, however, was loving the color and picked through the sizes in haste to get one on her body and to dispose of the purple flowered thing she arrived in. I'm grateful for that.

Since we both worked at the Palace last year, we knew the routine. We quickly eased into our roles of order-taker (Phoebe) and super-scooper (me). The line began to build as the dinner hour passed and vacationers finished their dinner next door. They headed into the shop for dessert, but Phoebe and I kept them all moving, happy and entertained with our singing to the Beach Boys tunes that were now heard loud and clear coming from The Crabby Tuna. The bands over there started up once the dinner crowd settled in, and now we were in for full entertainment for the rest of our shift. We belted out the words as if we were born and raised as California Girls in the sixty's, but that's the type of music that vacationers seemed to want while at the beach in New Jersey, so who were we to argue?

It wasn't long before I was up to my elbows in Mint Chocolate Chip and Blue Oreo when the door jingled and we saw Nick. Phoebe gave him a big smile, and I gave a nod as I concentrated on the pistachio-wafer-cone-with-rainbow-sprinkles that I was so carefully creating. Each cone to me was a masterpiece, and I took great pride in making sure that the scoops were artfully stacked on the cone, and the ice cream was thoroughly covered in the customer's covering of choice. Rainbow sprinkles were a favorite of mine, and I made sure that the extra nickel that was tacked onto the price of the cone for the sprinkles was well worth it.

As we got a lull in the orders, Nick approached and I noticed that there was someone tagging along with him. The blond god was lacking a tan at the moment, but I could tell his skin had seen the sun before, and his big brown eyes had a nice twinkle to them. He was about the same height as Nick, but was a bit more filled out; I guessed he was an athlete, as he seemed to carry himself with a bit more grace than Nick.

"Casey, this is Zack. I go to school with him up north. He's going to spend a few weeks here with me. Zack, Casey." Zack tried to extend his hand, but then reconsidered since mine were currently covered in all but two of the twenty-three flavors that the Polar Palace carried in their frozen cases. He put his hands into his shorts pockets to save grace.

"Hey, Zack, nice to meet you," I replied. "Can I get you something? A cone? Cup? Float?"

"Naah, I'm good. But thanks. Can I get you a napkin?" His eyes never left mine as he replied. *Hmmmm, what have we here? A guy with manners?*

"Oh, no, thanks, I have a towel back here somewhere." I turned and tried to locate the wash rags I used to clean up my hands in between masterpieces. By now Phoebe had made her way over for the Zack introduction and was already going through her twenty questions with him to assess how he knew Nick, where he lived, what his GPA was and how he kept the curl in his hair. She was relentless.

Nick saved him by interjecting, "I want to teach Zack how to wakeboard. Want to go tomorrow with us?" He directed the question to both Phoebe and me, and Phoebe answered for both of us before I could even get anything to form in my throat.

"Yes! That will be great! It's supposed to be another great day! What time?" I knew there was no way Phoebe would pass up spending time with Nick, so I nodded with agreement as Zack looked over at me. I do love wakeboarding, as it's another skill I am great at. I was sure I would be called on to give Zack a few lessons about how to water-start and how to jump the boat's wake.

"We're going to bike around for a bit, but we'll be back when you guys are off work." Nick winked at Phoebe. *What's this going on?*

"Bye, guys!" Phoebe said, directed to both but looking at Nick.

"Bye, Casey." Zack said to me, looking only at me.

Oh boy, this is going to get interesting.

Phoebe and I continued to take care of our customers while belting out the tunes that were wafting in from The Crabby Tuna. The Palace closed at 10 pm on the weekends, and we had about a half hour to go. Clean up after that was a breeze, since Phoebe's specialty is wiping down anything that moves. For the most part, the evening ran smoothly with just one mishap. A young boy decided that the vanilla cone his mother ordered for him wasn't as much fun to eat as the chocolate one his brother had. He threw it at his grandmother who tried to talk him down from his tirade. It ended up in her face, on her shirt, and on the lady sitting next to them who had just had her hair done for a wedding she had to attend the next afternoon. How did we know all this? She screamed it at the top of her lungs at the young boy's parents who seemed to want to disappear under the bench before anyone recognized them. After a brief visit from Cranberry Cove's finest men in blue, the matter was resolved and we were able to resume our duties without further incident.

With about five minutes to go before closing, Nick and Zack returned, greeted by the bell above the door, and our smiling faces.

"Almost ready to go?" Nick and Zack took a seat on the stool that Phoebe just wiped down.

"What are you guys up to?" Phoebe asked them both, as she headed over to the front door to flip the OPEN sign to CLOSED and flip the lock. Our shift had officially ended, and I headed to the sink to rid myself of the assorted sprinkles, caramel sauce and sticky goo that had accumulated during my evening's duties.

"Thought we'd just head up to the beach, you know, to...catch up," Nick said quietly. Zack looked on, as if he was fine with whatever plans were being made.

"Sounds great! We're in!" Phoebe once again answered for both of us.

"I just need to count out the register and then I'm ready. You all set Case?"

"Ummm, yeah, I'm good to go. Let me just get some refills here so the day crew is set for tomorrow." It's part of the duties of the night crew to make sure that the day crew has absolutely nothing to do when they get in. I think it's because the "newbies" get the day shift, and they would have no idea where anything was stored or what to do with it. The more experienced crew worked the night shift when the real crowds were in.

"I'll help you," Zack said as he followed me back to the storeroom before I could even protest. Once there, I directed him to a stack of medium-sized Styrofoam cups, a box of straws, and two boxes of napkins while I grabbed another tub of Tutti-Frutti and Chocolate Chip Cookie Dough to put into the freezer out front. Zack seemed nervous, and I wondered what he was up to. Could be that he was freaked out by the vibes Phoebe was giving off in anticipation of being up on the beach with Nick in a few minutes. Come to think of it, I was too. *Nick has no idea what he's in for...* I smiled to myself and directed Zack out of the storeroom and up front to put away our stash of supplies.

"Ready!" I announced as I slammed the freezer lid and headed over to the light switch. Phoebe had closed the register and Nick and Zack were waiting outside for us to emerge and head up to the beach. We grabbed our bikes from the rack, and me and my rusty old cruiser and Phoebe on her sherbet-colored Schwinn followed behind Nick and Zack, away from the Beach Boys playing at The Crabby Tuna, and up to where two other beach boys would soon be playing with us.

There is nothing like the beach at night. The sounds of the ocean waves breaking on shore, and the stillness of the night make for a very relaxing, almost spiritual experience. The beach is black — no lights at all — except for the moon shining over the water. Many of the vacationers will stay on the beach until around eight flying kites, watching their children build sandcastles, and just taking in the cool breezes. It is virtually empty, except for the few stargazers (lovers) who will venture up when it's dark to talk (ahem) and talk some more (ahem).

We parked our bikes at the bike rack that the Department of Public Works had so generously placed at the end of each beach block, and stepped onto the wooden planks of the boardwalk. The boardwalk runs the length of the town at the oceanfront. Many of the boards were recently engraved with family names and cutesy sayings from people who paid to "Buy a Board" in an effort to rebuild it — the boardwalk was destroyed by a massive hurricane a few years ago. The fundraiser was so successful, the town was able to have the boardwalk rebuilt at no cost to the taxpayers, all due to the generosity of the families and visitors who loved the town and wanted to help get it back to its original state. The boardwalk was now iconic, and people loved to walk the length of it, reading the sentiments of those who wanted so badly for it to be a part of their beach experience.

We walked a bit until we reached a path cut through the massive dunes. They were constructed to protect the homes from the ocean waves during the Nor'easters and hurricanes that frequent the east coast. We dropped our flip flops at the entrance (as is customary in Cranberry Cove) and walked onto the beach. None of us had uttered a word since we hopped onto our bikes; somehow we all knew that the quiet of the night was somehow sacred — loud voices would in some way be disrespectful to Mother Nature. We reached the end of the path and we saw the moon — full and enormous — greeting us like a beacon as it glowed low over the water in front of us.

Zack was the first to speak. "Holy.... Wow!" *Yup, that sums it up.*

We made our way about halfway down the beach towards the high tide line. That's the place where the sand changes from dry to wet because the waves at high tide will come higher up the beach then during the lower tide cycle. We plopped down together and just stared a moment. The sand was cool, and the sounds of crashing waves were all that could be heard.

"What a beautiful night." Phoebe made an observation.

"Yeah," Nick chimed in.

"Yup." That was Zack.

"How about that kid that threw the ice cream cone at that lady!" They all looked at me. I ruined the mood.

"Doofus," Phoebe said.

There is something to be said about being on the beach that first night of summer. You know it's the beginning of something really special, and a million things go through your mind as to what you are planning to do as the summer days go by. There is so much to do in Cranberry Cove: fishing, crabbing, sailing, wakeboarding, swimming, kayaking, biking, and of course, falling in love. It's every girl's dream to fall in love over the summer and then go back up north to tell your friends about the boy you left behind. Well, it's every girl's dream but mine. I'm perfectly okay with just minding my own business, having fun and waving to everyone else as they head up north in September. They go back to their other lives while I stay here on the island living mine. Heartbreak was something I never found to interest me, but Phoebe was certainly into living out that dream. Poor Nick was the one she set her sights on. Phoebe always got what she wanted.

Our quiet conversation began to focus on Zack. Turned out his parents were also divorced, and he met Nick when they both signed up for the school soccer team. Nick is just an average athlete; he'll try a little of this and a little of that to keep busy. Zack, however, according to Nick, is a natural. I knew that when I first laid eyes on him. He just moved with the grace of a guy that was comfortable with his body. He seemed to have muscles (I'll confirm that tomorrow when we wakeboard), and his legs are long. Really long. Like really long and nice. *Did I just say that?* His blond hair had a nice natural curl to it, not too long, not too short, with nice brown eyes and a great smile. *You already mentioned his eyes earlier.* In fact, I would say he was pretty good looking. Zack had just turned sixteen. I asked Zack how he liked Cranberry Cove so far.

"I like what I see so far. I'm sure I'll soon love it." *What does that mean?* His eyes looked right at mine as he spoke. He certainly had a way of communicating with those eyes.

For some reason, Phoebe and Nick seemed to be engaged in their own conversation. They had completely turned their backs on Zack and me. It wasn't long until Phoebe jumped up, her hand in Nick's, pulling him up to his feet as well.

"C'mon, Nick. Let's take a walk."

"Great!" Nick seemed a little too enthusiastic in his response, as he was able to translate "take a walk" to really mean "possibly make out behind the lifeguard stand."

"See you guys later — don't leave without us!" Phoebe ordered as she and Nick trotted off into the darkness towards the tipped over lifeguard stand. I looked over at Zack, who just sat quietly, probably wondering what the heck he was going to be subjected to now that the two of us were alone. I repositioned myself across from him to let him know right away that there would be no hanky-panky going on — THIS side of the lifeguard stand.

"So, have you ever gone wakeboarding before, Zack?"

"Nope, this will be my first time."

"Really? Wow." I looked down at my hand which was nervously digging a small hole to China in the sand next to me. "How are you at boogie boarding?"

"Never been."

"What??? You've never gone boogie boarding? How about body surfing?"

"Nope. Never." For the first time, he answered without looking right at me.

"Ever been in the ocean before?"

"Nope. My parents used to have a lake house, but since they divorced my mom doesn't really take me on vacations anywhere."

I keep forgetting that this is a vacation spot for most people, and I tend to take it for granted since I live here all year round. "Well, this is your lucky day! You've just met the person who is going to teach you the finer points of boogie boarding and body surfing! I hope you're up for it!" His huge smile and the sparkle in his beautiful brown eyes seemed to respond before his mouth opened with his reply.

"Great! I'm definitely up for it! When do we begin?"

"Well, our first lesson is wakeboarding tomorrow. The rest we'll cover after we master that. How long are you going to be in town?" And with that, Zack and I settled into a very comfortable, non-stressful, no-pressure discussion about the finer points of wakeboarding, boogie boarding and body surfing. Our conversation seemed natural and not forced, and I found myself actually enjoying his company. It turned out he is a lot like Nick, so there were many things we had in common. For example, he loves the METS (so do I), he despises the KNICKS (so do I) and we both think that while Daniel Craig makes a better James Bond than Pierce Brosnan, no one beats Roger Moore in that role. I think I've found my soulmate!

By 12:30 am, the bicycle cops noticed our cruisers were parked on the boardwalk and they strolled onto the beach to make sure we weren't getting ourselves into any trouble. Since the "Bike Cops" were actually college kids who aspired to be real cops one day, they knew the first place to look for errant teens on the beach at night was behind the tipped over lifeguard stand. So, they first ran across Nick and Phoebe who luckily were just holding hands and cuddling and talking. They informed Nick that he should probably "make sure the young lady gets home safely," which is cop-talk for "it's time to now leave the beach so we don't have to come up here looking for you later." The Bike Cops then walked over to us, followed by Nick and Phoebe, and proceeded to relay the same message.

"Casey?" I looked up at Bike Cop #1 with the baseball cap pressed down low over his eyebrows.

"Pauley?" *Oh, God* (under my breath, I swallow and stammer). "Hey, what's up?"

"Ummmm . . . everything okay here?" I guessed that was Pauley's way of making sure there was no non-consensual hanky-panky going on. His eyes slightly squinted, his left eyebrow up a bit, as he eyed Zack up and down, and calculated in his head the distance Zack was sitting from me and how far away his hands were from my . . . body.

"Oh, yeah, I'm good. This is Zack. Zack, this is my neighbor, Pauley."

Zack, gentleman that he was, thrusted his hand out to Pauley for a handshake.

"Nice to meet you, Zack. You know, it's getting late. You guys should be on your way."

"Yeah, you're right. We'll head out. Thanks, Pauley." Pauley was a nice guy, and he took his job seriously. He also liked my family. He felt a bit protective over me. I've known him since I was little, and he was always like the big brother I never had. I had no siblings, so Pauley used to teach me things — like how to bait a hook, or what wax to buy for my skim board. Pauley is actually credited with teaching me how to body surf. So, I can't fault the guy for giving Zack the once-over and the raised eyebrow as he summed up the situation.

"Have a good night, you two. And Zack, make sure she gets home safely."

"Yes, sir, I will." I laughed under my breath. I've never thought of Pauley as a "sir," but with his current position as a Class I Officer with the Cranberry Cove Police Force, he certainly had earned it. While he can't carry a gun, the word POLICE written across the back of his white polo shirt certainly lets everyone know that he was quick with a ticket book and carried a whistle and a radio. I know he'll make a great "real" cop one day, and his bike will be replaced by a full-fledged Cranberry Cove police cruiser.

The four of us headed to the pathway through the dunes and back to the boardwalk in silence. Out of the corner of my eye, I noticed Phoebe slip her hand into Nick's. *What's this? Public Display of Affection?* I'll definitely be asking about that later. We headed back to the bikes, and mounted them ready to ride home.

"Wakeboarding tomorrow?" Nick asked all of us.

"Definitely! I'm in!" Phoebe exclaimed enthusiastically.

"Me too!" Zack followed.

"Can we go for bagels first?" I whined.

"Doofus," I heard Phoebe mumble as we began our ride down the street.

Ten minutes later, text between Casey and Phoebe:

Casey: Well, what's the story?

Phoebe: What story? There is no story.

Casey: Yea right!

Phoebe: Nothing! hand-holding only

Casey: kiss?

Phoebe: Not yet.

Casey: ?

Phoebe: Awkward still.

Casey: Cool! A summer romance! On day one!

Phoebe: Yeah, Cool. See ya tomorrow for wakeboarding!

Casey: Zack's never been. I'm going to teach him.

Phoebe: OOOHH, summer romance!

Casey: Ummm. No.

Phoebe: Maybe?

Casey: Ummmm.. No.

Phoebe: Wear your one-piece.

Casey: Base Tan! Still need!

Phoebe: Don't be an doofus. Night!

Hmmm. Me and Zack? No way. I'm not looking for a summer romance. But he is kinda nice. And cute. And . . . and my mind drifted off into dreams of me and Zack and a long walk on the beach in July . . . .

"Casey, you are everything a Jersey Shore girl should be — smart, funny, tan and the best boogie boarder and ice cream scooper ever."

"Really? Why, Zack, you are the most handsome, sweetest, tannest North Jersey boy I've ever met. Please carry my beach chair for me? I want to see your big muscles protrude from under that tank top you are wearing."

"Oh, Casey, please let me kiss you. Smack! Slobber!" *What the . . .heck?*

"Sasha! Get off my bed!" I yelled at my Golden Doodle who had just returned from a romp along the bay. She had obviously decided to test the water and then run through the sand. She came back to the house to let me know all about it. Her coarse tongue cleaned any bit of drool that may have dripped down my chin from the dream I was just having about me and... Zack? *What?* I glanced at the clock. It's 9 am and I was reminded that today was wakeboarding day with Nick, Zack and Phoebe. We wanted to get onto the water before a lot of boat traffic appeared — it's easier for beginners to learn the sport on a flat bay, rather than a choppy one.

Text between Casey and Nick:

Casey: What time r we meeting?
Nick: 9:30 ok?
Casey: Good. Need anything?
Nick: Nope, all good.
Casey: Wanna fill me in on last night with Phoebes? :)
Nick: Nope, all good.
Casey: K see you there.
Casey: Zack excited?
Nick: Yup. Says Hi.
Casey: Hi Zack!
Nick: You used a !. I'm not yelling your Hi at him.
Casey: partypooper
Nick: See you in 30.
Casey: :)

Text between Phoebe and Casey:

Casey: We are meeting at 9:30
Phoebe: I know, heard from Nick already
Casey: Really? Sweet.
Phoebe: Duh
Casey: Real mature.
Phoebe: You should talk.
Casey: Duh
Phoebe: What are you wearing?

Casey: bathing suit

Phoebe: Duh

Casey: See you in 30.

Phoebe and I arrived with our bikes right at 9:30 to the street-end dock in town. For those residents who don't have houses that back up to the bay, there are a few boat slips that the town owns and rents. Nick's dad rents one of them for Nick's boat. After the divorce, in order to keep Nick from feeling his world was torn apart, his parents decided to try to substitute that there was no longer a family unit with a boat. It didn't work, but Nick does enjoy his boat. It's a used twenty-one foot Boston Whaler. It's very safe (his mom's requirement), with a single 150 hp outboard (his dad's requirement) and a Garmin fish-finder (Nick's requirement). Nick and his dad often go fishing in the bay for fluke, and in the ocean for stripers, sea bass, and ling. The fish-finder was a must. But the best thing about the boat is it came with a tow-rope and a wakeboard, and we've put those things to good use. Nick is a great captain, earning his license at fourteen as did many of the island kids because boating is such a part of living here in Cranberry Cove. Nick is also a great sailor, and his dad has a sixteen foot laser that we often take out on lazy days when we just want to enjoy the breeze and the bay (without the humming of a gas-powered motor in our ears). As family members of the Cranberry Cove Yacht Club, Nick's summer job has been instructing little kids on the fine art of sailing. He works there three days a week, and it's enough for him to make some spending money during the summer months.

Nick and Zack were already on the boat. He named it the Splitz in honor of the divorce. We were organizing the supplies we would need for the day: towels, the tow rope, the wakeboard, snacks *(bagels! yum!)*, and some beverages were all stowed and ready to accompany us on our adventure.

"Permission to board, Captain?" It's customary to always ask permission before boarding someone's boat. Nick looked at Phoebe and smiled.

"Absolutely, my lady!" Oh, boy. Phoebe just melted on that exchange. I followed behind, and as I prepared to jump from the finger dock onto the boat, Zack put out his hand for me to grab. He smiled and gave me a nod. *What a gentleman.* Phoebe was a bit put off at that gesture as Nick didn't make a move to help her get onto the boat. I'm sure that will be a topic of conversation later between us. She goes through her "I don't know, do you think he likes-likes me? Or just likes me?" discussion.

I turned to Zack as he settled into one of the seats at the stern. "Are you ready for this, Zack? You can swim, right? You'll need to float a bit, too. Think you can take a first step to becoming a full-fledged Jersey Beach Bum?"

"I'm ready. Are you? I understand you'll be teaching me."

"Yeah, I figured, since Nick will drive and Phoebe will spot." Whenever you do any watersports in the bay, such as wakeboarding or waterskiing, you need to have one driver and one spotter in the boat. The spotter just faces backward and informs the driver when the person falls. It's a law in Jersey. You also need an orange neon towing flag to be displayed on the boat — so other boaters will know to look out for the person in the water behind you.

Nick started up the engine, and with that, threw the boat into reverse and carefully backed us out of the slip. I decided to take a seat next to Zack since Phoebe innocently nestled next to Nick at the center console. Looked like I'd be spending a lot of time with Zack as the pairing off begins.

The morning was beautiful — no clouds, just a very slight breeze, but not one to kick up any waves, and very low humidity. Day two of the summer season was basically a perfect ten. We passed a couple of swans as we made our way towards the tiny bridge. It separated the island with a smaller island where the houses were just a bit bigger and the people were just a bit more... how shall we say... well off? There is a part of Cranberry Cove that was originally part of another township. The residents of the smaller island rallied to become part of the Cove because they are technically surrounded by us. You can't get there without driving through the Cove to get to the little bridge that connects us. So, as nice as we Covers are, we took them into our fold and now they are us... sort of. We have a few celebrities that have houses there, and it's a favorite bike riding route among the tourists to see if they can spot any of them out and about in their yards.

We reached the bridge and waved to the little kids throwing out a fishing line from under its shadows. They attempted to catch a snapper or two. We followed the channel to a quiet area of the bay behind the town's bayfront gazebo to begin to take our first run. The plan was to have me take the first turn, explain to Zack how to float in the water, how to hold the line, how to pull up as the boat begins to tug the line, and then how to signal the spotter to speed up or slow down. It's all the basic stuff you would do when wakeboarding or waterskiing.

Nick pulled around and put the boat into neutral. We virtually stopped and floated. He and Zack began to attach the tow rope to the stern of the boat and put the tow flag up. Phoebe and I made our way to the bow of the boat to take off the shorts and shirt I threw on over my bathing suit. I pulled off my t-shirt when Phoebe let out a gasp.

"Where's the one-piece? Casey, you were supposed to wear the one-piece!"

I looked at her with a scowl. "I told you last night I'm still working on my base tan. What's the big deal?"

"The big deal," she said as she poked a finger into my chest for emphasis, "is that you are going to flash everyone, including Nick and Zack, once you take a spill off that board! I thought we talked about this?"

Now she added a foot stomp to further emphasize — her voice ended up with a bit of a whine to it.

"I am not going to fall — don't worry about that. I'm good at this!" Now she'd basically given me the kiss of death. I knew eventually this wasn't going to turn out as planned. But, there was no way I would be wearing a t-shirt when I am on that board. I needed to work on my base tan!

"Okay, they're your boobs, not mine out there. Remember that!" She shook her head and waved her hand to dismiss me and the conversation. Man, she gets really hung up on this topic.

"Don't worry about that, I'll remember!" I dissed her back.

I moved to the back of the boat as Nick was giving Zack some background on how the boat's electronics worked. Nick had a great fish-finder on the boat that he used in the ocean, but in the bay it didn't really work well. It's just too shallow. I took over the conversation as I began to toss the wakeboard into the water behind the motor. I rested my foot on it to keep it close as I straddled the stern and put on my life jacket.

"Okay, Zack. Remember to keep clear of the prop on the engine. Keep the rope with you, or else you'll be chasing after it as it drifts away. The board is very floaty, so once your feet are in it, it will be awkward. But just relax and don't panic and you'll find your center." I zipped up my life jacket, which is required wear for anyone getting towed; I plopped off the back of the boat and into the water. Phoebe tossed me the tow line, and I let the boat drift slowly away from me as I held onto the board with one hand and the rope with the other. The life jacket was floaty enough and was holding me up nicely. I was actually very relaxed in this position.

I placed my feet in the rubber slots on the wakeboard and it floated in front of me. Laying on my back, feet up, I swung the tow rope to the front of me to get ready to give the signal to Phoebe to have Nick pull forward. Zack was looking at me in wonder as I continued to float further from the stern of the boat. I got into my comfortable position, and raised my hand to signal for Nick to put the boat into drive to move forward.

As Nick gave the boat just a little gas, I saw the Splitz move further away. The tow line that was wrapped in waves and circles in the water was now beginning to straighten out — I prepared myself for the tug and lurch that would occur once the line was pulled taut. Once I saw it was going to happen, I leaned just a bit forward and prepared to hold tight. The line was completely taut now, and I felt myself being tugged forward. I stretched out my legs with perfect timing as Nick continued to press down the throttle and increase the speed. In a flash, I was standing on the board, flying behind the boat. I noticed a complete look of awe flash across Zack's face as he watched from the stern.

I'm in my element. I love everything about the water, whether it's bay or ocean. I could do this all day, breeze in my hair, water splashing around me, smile plastered across my cheeks. I get lost in thought out here and it's as if I'm in a kind of suspended animation — on autopilot — as my knees buckle to absorb the shocks from the small wake made from the boats movement.

Nick made a slow turn, and I gave the hand signal to Phoebe to have him increase the speed. It was exhilarating as I began to weave a bit, showing off my skills to Zack; he was obviously impressed by my talent. I weaved left out of the flat water and jumped over the wake of the Splitz, then back right across the wake to the other side where I gracefully jumped that wake as well. I dropped one hand from the tow rope to push the hair from my eyes and I saw Zack raise an eyebrow. Obviously that move also impressed him. All was going well, until from the corner of my eye, I saw a guy on a Jet Ski racing towards me.

I see Jet Skis on the bay as water mosquitos. The people who ride them are usually careless, and think they are the only motor powered crafts out there. Because they are so easily maneuvered, the drivers like to do wheelies, make circles and bounce them around. The problem for real boat captains is that you can't anticipate what moves they are going to make. Captains rely on reading the subtleties of other craft's movements to commit to safe passage around other boats. With Jet Ski riders, well, you don't know what they are thinking — they just seem to run around like, well, like water mosquitos.

   This particular Jet Ski driver was not making eye contact with me. I wanted to get his attention to give him a warning to back away a bit, but he seemed to just have an eye on the boat's wake — his goal was to jump it. The problem was that if he didn't keep an eye on Nick and where Nick was planning to turn, I may end up tangled up with this guy. I started to wave my hand to get his attention. Now Phoebe, my spotter, saw the Jet Ski Guy as well. And, she saw me waving. She misread my signal as an okay for Nick to go faster. For Nick to accelerate he had to turn and head back the other way. He didn't know that Jet Ski Guy was coming on fast and furious. Nick began to turn. Jet Ski Guy was only watching the wake the boat was leaving, licking his chops as to how high it was going to take him when he jumped it. Nick completed the turn. Jet Ski Guy jumped the wake. I hit the boat wake. I hit Jet Ski Guy's wake. I launched. I face planted into the water. All I saw was black. All I heard was garbled sound. I emerged. Seaweed was on my head, along with my bathing suit top.

   I tried to get my bearings. Jet Ski Guy floated up and asked if I was alright. I gave him an earful.

   "DOES IT LOOK LIKE I'M ALRIGHT? JEEZ, WHAT IS YOUR PROBLEM? DIDN'T YOU SEE HIM TRYING TO TURN? WHAT IS IT WITH YOU NUTCASES ON THESE JET SKIS? DIDN'T YOU HAVE TO TAKE A SAFETY COURSE OR SOMETHING?" I continued to spew things at him; all the while my head was covered with seaweed and a yellow and blue bikini top. Luckily, my lifejacket had saved my life, and kept the girls under wraps.

   Nick turned the boat around and floated up to where Jet Ski Guy and I were having it out. Nick began to pick up where I left off, while Zack motioned me over to the back of the boat and to safety. I was okay, but my ego was bruised. I was doing great out there before this happened. Zack reached over the boat and gently removed the bathing suit top and the seaweed from the top of my head. All I heard was Nick yelling, Jet Ski Guy apologizing, and Phoebe with her classic response. "Doofus," she said. I looked up at Zack. He grabbed my arms and hoisted me up onto the boat. Then he spoke. "You are the champion," he said as he looked me right in the eyes. *Yes, yes I am.* Lesson over.

I must be a good teacher because I was pretty impressed with how quickly Zack had picked up the skill of wakeboarding. After a few tries and losing the tow rope a couple of times as Nick accelerated, Zack seemed to get the hang of it and was able to cruise around the bay for a good ten minute run before he would drop the line and cruise into a soft water landing. Each time we circled around to pick him up, he'd ask to try it again. I noticed that Zack didn't like to fail, and wanted to keep going until he felt he had mastered it.

Phoebe and I sat in the back of the boat, eating our bagels, spotting together, and admiring the view. Phoebe was into admiring Nick at the helm, but I kept my eye on Zack. He really was a good looking guy I noticed. I guess I noticed too much, because before long I was poked in the arm by someone next to me.

"Hello! Earth to Casey! Didn't you hear anything I said?"

"Wh-hat? No, I was spotting."

"Spotting my butt! You are so checking him out! You like him! You like Zack..."

"Ummmm . . . no."

"Ummmm . . . yes."

"Ummm . . . no."

"Yes you do, Casey, you haven't taken your eyes off of him."

"I'm not supposed to! I'm spotting! You should talk! YOU are supposed to be spotting!"

Phoebe looked at me, smiled and said almost apologetically, "I know. I think I'm really falling for Nick. Can you believe it? Think he likes me?" Here we go. I knew this conversation was going to happen sooner or later.

"Yes, he likes you. Can't you tell?"

"But does he like-like me or just like me?"

"He like-likes you!"

"You sure?"

"You are the doofus, Phoebe!" I took a bite of my bagel and turned back to Zack. This conversation was now over.

After about another hour of Zack in the water, we convinced him to come in to "de-prune." He was shriveled up, but filled with pride at how well he had done on the bay all morning. By now it was nearing noon, and the boat traffic was beginning to increase, and it just wasn't safe to be wakeboarding anymore. We promised him we'd do it again while he was in town. He seemed appeased.

Nick drove us over to the Cranberry Cove Yacht Club for lunch. It's not a hoity-toity yacht club like you see in magazines in the Caribbean or in the movies. It's just a huge old wooden house with a red roof and a big outside porch and deck where people sit while their children and grandchildren are taking sailing lessons. Women play mahjong on the deck and the men play cards. Members stop in for lunch or dinner, or to take out their sailboats. On some summer nights, they hold dances or special activities for the members. But no one dresses up in anything but what seems to be Cranberry Cove's official uniform: shorts, t-shirts, bathing suits, flip flops. We are very casual here in Cranberry Cove.

Nick pulled into a slip and Zack and I helped to steady the Splitz and tie her up to the pilings. Zack jumped out and put a hand out for me, but I couldn't go until I grabbed my bathing suit top, which I hadn't yet been able to put back on, so I was still wearing my life jacket. Zack smiled as I showed him that I now had it, and was ready to disembark. I hopped off, followed by Phoebe and then Nick. The captain is always the last one off. *I guess that's why they always seem to go down with the ship.*

I gestured to Phoebe that I was going to go to the ladies' room to put my top back on. She seemed to understand, and decided to come with me. She motioned to Nick to grab a table while we were gone.

I love going inside the Yacht Club building. It's filled with old photos hanging on the wall, and nautical flags and memorabilia of a time past when people did get dressed up to come here. It's something that makes Cranberry Cove special, as the older buildings in town are really few and far between now. All of the buildings and houses around town seemed to be getting knocked down and replaced by newer, bigger buildings, and that connection to the past, to days that were simpler and easier, was disappearing. So the Yacht Club building is special that way. The view from the porch is beautiful as you can scan the entire bay and watch the sails of the boats puff out as the wind carries them across the water. There is a little island that sits just off the side porch that is a sanctuary and nesting ground for seagulls. You see them flying around the tiny island. You see the puffy baby birds as they venture out for their first flight, learning to catch minnows, spearing, and baby crabs. They screech like crazy when a kayaker or boat approaches too closely.

Phoebe and I took care of business in the ladies' room, and emerged hungry and ready for lunch with the guys. As we approached the table, we saw Zack animatedly reliving every ride he took as Nick looked intently at him. Nick missed most of the action because he had to face forward while driving the boat, so Zack made sure not one detail was missed.

"The waitress is bringing out Cokes for us, but we didn't order yet," Nick said while Zack was still reliving his adventure. I made my way to one of the strategically placed open chairs at the round table which would make for a boy-girl-boy-girl seating arrangement. *How clever of them.* I reached to grab the back of the chair to pull it out when Zack jumped out of his chair and proceeded to pull the chair out for me! I was stunned for a second, but then smiled and thanked him. As I sat, I looked at Phoebe, who had to pull her own chair out and wasn't happy about it.

It's hard to imagine what is going on inside a guy's head at this age. I can't even imagine what they think goes on in ours. In fact, there is NO WAY they would ever be able to figure it out. But guys are different. They are genetically engineered to try to attract a female, and there aren't too many guidebooks out there for teenage boys to help them out. They rely on what they see on television shows (heaven help us!) and in movies (help us again!), and maybe older brothers (eee-gad!) but other than that, they are helpless creatures trying to make their way. So, for Zack to be pulling out the gentlemanly manners thing, I knew he was really trying to make an impression. And it's actually working. I never thought I'd say it, but I just may end up this summer with my own "boy-I-left-behind" story. *Hmmmm . . . we'll see.*

After a Sunday night of slinging ice cream at the Polar Palace, which was preceded with a day full of fun and frolic on Nick's boat, the chilly Monday morning rain was actually a pleasant surprise. It gave me some time to just cuddle up in bed and rest my aching muscles, and allowed me to re-examine the battle scars from Saturday's epic bodysurfing session. The island was filling up with vacationers, and now with today's rain, I imagined that the local movie theaters and stores would enjoy the vacationers' wallets. It was all part of living in a tourist area — everyone wanted a piece of the action, and the weather played a huge role in who would benefit. On a sunny day, the local stores selling all types of beach attire and accessories would win out, but on a rainy day the local malls and movie theaters would be on the winning end. Rain usually cut down on the amount of visitors we would get at the Polar Palace, but it didn't matter to me right now, as it was my day off. All I wanted to do was relax.

Sasha had already been out to do her business, so my room had that homey scent of "wet dog." She was cuddled up at the foot of my bed, most likely enjoying the morning as I was, and snoozing comfortably. I used the remote to flip aimlessly through the morning talk shows, news and Maury Povich. *People actually watch this stuff?* I settled in as the topic grabbed my interest: GUYS WHO LOVE GIRLS THAT HAVE WEIRD TATTOOS. My attention immediately focused on a girl with tattoos all over her face and neck and body, easily seen because she also had a tattoo that looked like a two-piece bathing suit. Other than the bathing suit tattoo, she was totally naked. I was mesmerized. *Could this be the answer to my bathing suit dilemma?* I immediately picked up my phone and texted Phoebe.

Text between Casey and Phoebe:

Casey: Turn on channel 11! Quick!

Phoebe: *no response*

Casey: Phoebes! Hurry Up! Channel 11!

Phoebe: *no response*

Casey: I'm calling you!

Phoebe: Don't call! How can I text you when I'm running to get in front of the TV? What am I watching?

Casey: Check out the chick in the bathing suit.

Phoebe: The one with the tattoos?

Casey: Yeah. Notice anything?

Phoebe: a lot of tattoos.

Casey: anything else?

Phoebe: more tattoos and the guy is drooling.

Casey: No! look at the bathing suit!

Phoebe: What is it?

Casey: The answer to my problem.

Phoebe: *no response*

then ...

Phoebe: doofus

Casey: just kidding! lol

Phoebe: so what should we do today? mall?

Casey: how about movies? Zack and Nick?

Phoebe: you wrote Zack's name first... oooohhhhhh

Casey: now who's the doofus?

Phoebe: okay, I'll text Nick to set something up.

Casey: okay, heading back to bed for a bit. I ache.

Phoebe: for Zack?

Casey: blah blah blah keep me posted.

Phoebe: k

I looked at the bathing suit tattoo once more and then changed the channel. *SpongeBob! Now here's some entertainment!*

The noon movie was packed. We decided to go with a comedy because no one wanted to see Phoebe's romantic movie and Phoebe and I refused to see anything that involved robots and space. The comedy was at least something we could all agree on. Since none of us drove yet, we had to get a lift from Phoebe's brother, Jase, who didn't have to lifeguard because of the rain. It was a bit awkward, being I had a crush on him and all, but I made sure when we all crammed into the car that I called "shotgun" so I could sit next to him. I didn't want him wondering if I was at all connected to Nick or Zack romantically, which I wasn't, although Zack's charms were becoming more difficult for me to ignore.

The awkwardness was now about to begin. I sensed it. First of all, it's not a date when everyone pays separately. But the boys, of course, were looking for this opportunity to stake a claim on us, so to speak, so they were taking this chance seriously. It was a crazy race to the ticket window once we poured out of the car. Three of us raced to the window in an effort to set the tone for the day, except for Phoebe, who slowly climbed out of the car and sauntered behind us. She wanted Nick to take charge and buy her a ticket. That would confirm to her that he like-liked her. Nick seemed okay with it, and he flung a $20 bill at the girl in the booth and requested two tickets. Phoebe beamed. Nick beamed. Nick gathered his change and they headed over to the concession stand. Now Zack stepped up. "Two please," he told the girl.

"Zack, you don't have to, I can get my own ticket," I whispered as I touched his arm lightly with my fingertips. *Why did I do that?*

"Please, Casey, it's the least I can do for all the time you spent teaching me to wakeboard yesterday. I insist."

"Well, then I'm getting the popcorn," I stated with a smile and a flitter of my eyelashes. *Why did I do that?*

"Deal."

I had no idea why my stomach was now in a tizzy. I guess it's because at that moment it hit me: this was an official, no way out, can't deny it, date. I glanced at Phoebe as we headed over to the concession stand to meet up. Zack stood up next to Nick, Phoebe pulled me aside.

"What is up with you? You look like a deer in the headlights! Lighten up!"

"Zack bought my ticket."

"I know! I was watching! How cool!" She giggled and grabbed my arms.

"Phoebes, I just don't know about this! I'm okay with Zack outside, but this is a dark movie theater! What if he tries something?" I tried to keep my voice low.

"OOhhhh, can you imagine? How great! He's cute, Casey, enjoy it!"

I gritted my teeth at her. Her excitement was something I just didn't share right now. "Phoebes! Snap out of it! I'm serious here!"

"What can happen? A yawn and an arm over your shoulder? No one makes out in a theater anymore, Casey. They did that when your parents were young. This will be a cuddle fest at the most. Maybe some hand-holding. No big deal."

Not that I'm a prude by any means — I've read my share of romantic beach-reads where boys and girls meet and fall in love and kiss and all that. I'm just not sure I'm ready for it all. It's fine when it happens to characters in a book, but I'm not sure how fine I'll be with it as Casey of Cranberry Cove. *Hmmmm… a good title for book…*

The line at the concession stand began to inch forward, and our group was almost at the front. The next test for Phoebe was going to be whether Nick purchased one or two bags of popcorn. Two meant he was thoughtful, but one meant he was "thoughtful," in other words he put some thought into what one bag of popcorn meant. You see, buying one bag would cause Phoebe to have to sit close to Nick in order to get at the popcorn, and there would always be the chance that their hands would touch if they both reached into the bag at the same time. Trust me — Phoebe was really noticing every move Nick made to try to better understand Nick's view of this relationship. The moment of truth was revealed when Nick purchased one large bag of popcorn and one large soda. As soon as Phoebe heard the order Nick gave to the guy with the paper hat on, she turned to me and mouthed, "O-M-G!" She could barely contain herself. She slipped her arm through Nick's as he paid the cashier, grabbed the popcorn and handed it over to Phoebe with a smile, took the soda, and then picked up two straws from the dispenser. I saw Phoebe's shoulders sag just a bit. Oh, well, I guess Nick felt sharing a straw was just a bit too cozy yet. *Two steps forward, one step back.* With that setback, Phoebe followed Nick, still with her arm in the crook of his elbow, off to the side to wait while my fate was determined.

Zack stepped up to the counter, as the guy in the paper hat and two palms on the glass countertop said, "What'll it be?" Zack turned to me.

"Sharing okay with you?"

"Hey," I countered, "I thought I was buying the popcorn?"

"I'd like to get it, if that's okay with you. Can I treat?" It was actually kind of sweet that instead of Zack being all cave-man-like, he actually *asked* if he could get the snacks for the movie. His eyes pleaded with mine, and I found myself staring back, unable to speak. His eyes were... mesmerizing. His hair fell softly upon his forehead, his cheeks rosy pink from yesterday's sun, his lips...

"Ummm, I don't have all day here, folks — I have a line out past the restrooms. So what will it be?"

I snapped out of my trance. "Ooh, ahh, yeah, Zack, that's fine. Thank you." I stumbled on the words, and watched Zack carefully as he paid the guy with the paper hat, grabbed the popcorn and soda, and grabbed ONE straw from the dispenser. *Oh boy, this is getting interesting...*

The movie theater was pretty packed, but we managed to make our way to four seats that were off to the right side. I was happy about that, because if there was any cuddling to be going on, I certainly didn't want it to be funnier than the comedy that would be showing on the screen. Nick walked into the aisle first, followed by Phoebe, then me, and then Zack. It was a row of five seats, so it was unlikely that anyone would sit next to Zack. The rows were angled toward the screen, and although there were people in the rows behind us, we were fortunate that the row directly behind us was empty. At least that left a bit of a buffer for what I felt was an awkward situation waiting to happen.

As soon as we were seated, the lights went down and the previews began. Phoebe and I have this thing we do during the preview section. After each one, we rate it by giving a thumbs up or thumbs down, and rank it on a scale of one to ten. A thumbs up with a rank of ten is a must-see, and a thumbs down with a rank of one is a definite miss. Anything in the four to six range is a possibility, and if we are desperate and really bored, we would consider seeing it. Since they play about ten previews in this particular theater, Phoebe and I sat up ready to thumb and rank the previews.

The first one came on. It was set in space, and showed what looked like a space colony. I immediately shot up my thumbs down sign before the first scene even changed. "What are you doing?" Zack whispered, gesturing with his chin at my hand in the air.

"I'm ranking the preview," I stated matter-of-factly.

"Why?"

"To show whether or not I'd want to see it. Don't you ever do it?"

"Ummm, no, I just don't go see it if I don't like it."

"Oh. This seems to be more fun." I smirked.

"You don't like space movies?"

"Not really, do you?"

"Yeah, I think they're okay. I like the idea of being out in the unknown."

"Oh, yeah, I guess I do, too." And slowly, I watched in horror as my thumbs down began to slowly turn to the side and before you know it, it was pointing right up to the gum-covered ceiling as if it had a mind of its own!

"What are you doing? You hate space movies!" Phoebe whispered over to me out of the corner of her mouth.

"I know, I mean, I don't know. Zack likes them and I guess he just talked me into that one." My words were weak and filled with fear at what was becoming of me while I sat next to this hunk of a guy, my insides in turmoil, my eyes clouded over with . . . with . . . lust.

"Oh boy, you know what we've got here?" Phoebe asked although not really a question. "You've got a case of the smittens! You like him!"

Phoebe was pinching my leg and knocking me with her shoulder, so hard that I in turn smacked into Zack.

"You okay over there?" I heard Zack whisper to me.

"Ummm, yeah, sorry. I must have gotten a chill." It was the first thing that popped into my head to explain why I almost knocked him into the empty seat next to him.

"Why didn't you say so?" And with that, he lifted his arm and put it over my head and wrapped it around my seat, resting his hand on my shoulder. I looked at Phoebe, and her mouth was hanging wide open, eyes wide, fingers with a piece of popcorn hung in mid-air right in front of her face. My face? Picture deer in headlights, second time in the last thirty minutes.

She turned to Nick. "I'm cold, too!"

"Yeah, the air's on a bit high. Told you to bring a sweatshirt." Nick continued to eat his popcorn.

Phoebe humphed into her seat. *Two steps forward, one step back.*

The movie was hysterical, and I sat with Zack's arm around my shoulder, sharing a popcorn and soda with one straw, enjoying the company of this hunk of a guy. Next to me, Phoebe was trying everything she could to get Nick to make a move on her, either to hold her hand or wrap his arm around her. With about ten minutes left in the movie, poor Nick looked to finally have the courage to throw his arm around the back of Phoebe's chair. She finally relaxed, and sunk down with a smile on her face. Zack and I finished our popcorn, giggled and whispered, and when the lights came up and the credits began to roll on the screen, I felt a tinge of sadness that this experience would now come to an end.

"What a great movie!" Phoebe crooned, no doubt her words actually in direct correlation to the fact that Nick finally made the move on her.

"It was great," Zack smiled, eyes on me, comfortable in his self-confidence. He removed his arm from the seat, did a bit of a two-armed stretch and yawn, and then immediately put it back. "What's next on the agenda?" He seemed to ask to no one in particular.

"Mall for a bite to eat?" I jumped in, trying to contribute in any way I could to keep this now-approved "date" from ending. The movie theater was free-standing, but shared the parking lot with the mall, so it would just be a short walk over to get to the indoor stores and restaurants.

"Sounds good to me!" Zack huffed as he popped up from his seat, and held his hand out for me to hold. Without hesitation, I grabbed it. We snaked our way through the crowd, into the theater lobby, and out the front door heading in the direction of the mall. Once outside, Zack and I seemed to float as we led the way, glancing at each other, talking about the movie, and swinging our connected arms in a beautiful rhythm that seemed to scream "summer love." To me, it felt sweet. To Phoebe, it was nauseating. Nick's hands were in his hoodie pockets, seemingly oblivious to Phoebe's attempts of affection. Finally, she snaked her arm through his, resting it on the crook of his elbow, and eased into a stroll next to Nick. Nick looked at her and smiled, and all was well with the world again.

Being with Zack that afternoon was like stepping into heaven — warm and bright, light and easy, and very comfortable. The butterflies in my stomach seemed to settle down, and we laughed and talked through lunch at the Burger Barn, and even walked through Rick's Sporting Goods and the Water Wrangler to look at the latest in swimwear, kayaks, wakeboards and boogie boards. Nick checked out the latest boating accessories, and purchased a fishing magazine which highlighted the best hot spots in the area for nailing the big ones.

Phoebe called Jase to pick us up around 4:30. Since the rain had stopped by then, we waited outside for our ride at the park benches that were scattered around the entrance. Jase arrived about ten minutes after Phoebe's call, and pulled right up to where we were sitting. Nick and Phoebe piled into the back. Zack also climbed into the back. To do so, he had to drop my hand. Immediately, I sensed a feeling of loss. *Oh, man, did I just feel sad?* I climbed in shotgun, and after buckling my seatbelt, I realized that we weren't moving. I glanced over at Jase, who was just looking at me with a smirk on his lips. I stared back. "How was the movie, Beach Girl?"

"Good. Real good. Funny. It was . . . funny."

He continued to stare. And smirk. It was then I realized that he saw Zack and me holding hands. *Oh crap.*

"C'mon, Jase. What's the holdup?" Phoebe cried out from the back seat. I glanced over the seat back. I didn't know what was up her butt since she was now sandwiched between two good looking studs in the back seat.

"Alright, I'm going," Jase mumbled, and with one more glance at me and a smirk, he pulled out towards the exit of the mall parking lot.

I sat in silence. Was he making fun of me? Was he upset that I was holding hands with Zack? Was my fly open? My mind was reeling. I sat, looking straight ahead as he drove us home. The whole car was quiet, except for the song that happened to be playing on the local beach radio station, "Summer Nights" from Grease. *What a coincidence*, I thought to myself. I felt my cheeks flush with heat.

Nick's dad was taking Nick and Zack out for dinner that night, so Phoebe and I just hung inside at my house for the evening. She came over after she ate with her family, and parked herself in my room. Of course the conversation drifted immediately into what happened at the movie theater.

"I just don't get what's going on with Nick. One minute he acts like he likes me, and then I'm practically throwing myself at him to make him pay attention to me. Is he thick? Do I need to hit him over the head with a brick or something?" Phoebe was beside herself. She just couldn't figure this one out. Short of putting a neon sign on top of her head that says PHOEBE LOVES NICK, along with a few bottle rockets and Roman candles shooting out from her ponytail, she was running out of ideas as to how to get him to loosen up with her. "And you, all you do is tell Zack you have a chill and he's throwing his arm around you like he's putting out a fire! Why does he get it, and Nick doesn't?"

"I don't know, Phoebes. Maybe you are trying too hard. Maybe Nick just doesn't know how to act around you anymore. He's always been part of our threesome, and now this romantic twist is confusing him. He's probably just scared. Who knows what goes on in a guy's head?" Actually, I understood Nick's confusion as I was suffering from the same thing. I never asked to have Zack come into my life. My life was perfect as it was. But now I was feeling all kinds of weird things that are pretty scary. I didn't want my heart broken, and from what I've heard that's where summer romances always end up. No one can successfully pull off the "long distance romance" at our age. It just has never been done. "You know, I never asked Zack to like me. And who knows? Maybe he's just using me for the few weeks he's here and has no intention to take it any further. I mean, c'mon, look at me. I'm no beauty queen. I'm a loud, obnoxious, so-far-from-feminine beach girl who likes to pick up dead crabs and run people over with a boogie board. I'm certainly not what a North Jersey guy would ever be able to bring home to his mom. I don't have big hair, wear makeup, and I don't have an accent. I'm an alien!"

"That's probably what he's attracted to," Phoebe mumbled, adding, "You are everything that those other girls aren't. But to Nick, I'm just like the other girls he sees, so what's the big deal? Ugh, let's face it, I can't compete with the other girls either." In defeat, she buried her face in my pillow, and screamed loudly.

"Ummm . . . feel better? You didn't slobber on it, did you?" I asked, smiling, trying to bring her out of this emotional breakdown that she was on the verge of having.

"No, no slobber. But I'm still upset! I am not leaving this summer without becoming Nick's official girlfriend! Casey, you have to help me! Talk to him!"

"WHAT? No way, Oh, no! I'm not getting involved in that — no way! This is your deal. Maybe you just need to take it a bit slower, make it a little less obvious. You know, play hard to get? I hear that works with guys. In the book I'm reading, the girl liked this guy and he didn't . . ."

"Ugh! Enough with your beach reads! This isn't a romantic fiction story with a cover that has a beach and an umbrella and a bright sunshine and two people holding hands. This is reality, Casey!" *Man, how did she know what I was reading?*

"Look, Phoebe. I have no idea why Nick is playing this the way he is. Maybe he just doesn't know what to do? Maybe he hasn't had a girlfriend before. Give him some time to figure it out. We have all summer. Why rush it?" She glanced at me as I spoke, as if she was really taking in my words. Then, she put her head back into my pillow and screamed again. She picked her head up, and gingerly positioned herself at the edge of the bed, taking a deep breath as if to calm herself.

"Okay, I am calm now. I am calm now. I am calm now," she chanted as if talking herself into it. Our eyes met. She smiled. I smiled. My phone buzzed. A text from Zack.

Text between Zack and Casey:

Zack: Hey beautiful. Just saying hi. *(he thinks I'm beautiful!)*
Casey: Hi! *(did that sound too anxious?)*
Zack: Gonna be around later?
Casey: Phoebes and I are at my house.
Zack: Nick and I are out, but home around 9. Ice cream?
Casey: Sure! Nick and Phoebe too?
Zack: Let me check. *(Uh oh…. C'mon Nick…)*
Zack: Yes.
Casey: Great! text when you are back.

"See? I told you just to give it a chance. We're going for ice cream at nine."

"Why didn't Nick text me?" A lilt of sadness showed in Phoebe's voice.

"I guess because Zack texted. I told him you were here."

Phoebe sighed. "I have my work cut out for me."

"Don't sweat it. Things will happen. Just play it cool. Let's see what happens tonight."

With that she threw herself back onto my bed, and buried her head in my pillow for yet another scream.

At 8:45 pm, the text from Zack came through to let us know that they were back and ready for dessert. Of course, Phoebe's idea of dessert was probably different than Nick's at this point, but that didn't matter right now. What was important was that Phoebe was going to get Nick to notice her as something more than part of our trio, and she was anxious to get started. So, she hopped on her sherbet-colored bicycle, and I jumped on my rusty steel one, and we headed out. Our destination? The Broadway Beltway Singing Ice Cream Shoppe.

This place is a great time.

The entire staff at Broadway Beltway is dressed in old-time candy striper/barbershop quartet type outfits — right down to the saddle shoes. After you are seated, your order is taken by a singing waiter while upbeat music is blaring out of the overhead speakers. You can't help but sing along. When your ice cream arrives, you're forced to do something for it. By do something, I mean make a fool of yourself. You sing some crazy song lyric, do a crazy dance, or act out some Broadway show scene, all while drooling over the sundae that you can see, but can't touch . . . yet. Of course, the entire restaurant is filled with people watching and hoping that their fate won't be as embarrassing. When you are done, everyone cheers, and you dig into your sundae while some other unsuspecting victim does their penance.

It's traditional to get the person in your group who's never been through this before to order the one item that you know will be picked on the worst. So, that was going to be Zack. We talked him into ordering the sundae that would take him to the front of the restaurant to participate in this crazy rap/cheer while wearing a wig of pigtails and throwing his arms around wildly with rainbow colored pom poms. I believe the cheer also had the words "super duper ice cream scooper" in it.

While we waited for our fate and our sundaes to arrive, I looked at Zack and inquired about dinner. "So, how was your evening out?" I asked, his brown eyes gazing into mine as he hung on every word coming from my mouth.

"Great. I am so stuffed! Nick's dad really knows where to get a great steak." I smiled at Zack and his enthusiasm for the great meal he enjoyed, watching as he patted his stomach with his right hand, while he smoothly moved his left hand to the back of my chair. Yes, it was a smooth move. I also noticed how the move was not lost on Phoebe, who watched with awe. I kind of felt bad for her. I made a mental note to ask Zack later what he thought of the Nick-Phoebe situation. Our table conversation focused on what was going on around us: the kids laughing, the customers who were called on to sing or chant, and what our favorite ice cream toppings were. It wasn't that long before our table was approached by a cute waitress in a red and white apron, holding a large sundae high above her head.

"Ladies and Gentlemen," her voice rang out. "Someone at this table ordered a super-duper-banana-chocolate-caramel-sundae! Would that person please meet me at the front of the restaurant?" Oh, boy. Here it was. Zack's big moment. I looked at him and he froze. But trooper that he was, he got up out of his seat and winked at me *(he winked!)* before following the waitress, and his sundae, to the front of the room.

"What's your name?" asked the waitress.

"Zack."

"Well, Zack, you look like the athletic type. Have you ever cheered before?"

"Ummm, no," he laughed and blushed and looked at our table and shook a fist at us in jest for getting him into this situation. We were all smiles as we enjoyed with great anticipation the awkward moment that all in the restaurant were about to witness.

"Well, Zack, I'd like you to put on this wig, and this skirt, and hold onto these pom poms." As everyone giggled and laughed, Zack played along like the good sport he was. He was really enjoying this, and enjoying that we were as well. Zack slipped on the oversized cheerleader skirt, plopped the blonde wig of pigtails onto his head and held onto the pom poms.

"Okay, Zack, now watch me. Ready?" The waitress turned to the audience and went into full high school cheerleader mode. She grabbed a pair of pom poms from a box on the floor, and began clapping them together in a rhythm as she chanted, "Caramel is sweet, bananas are long, my super-duper ice cream scooper made me sing this song!" And with that, she threw her arms up in the air and twirled them around cheerleader style while putting on a big fake smile and ending up kneeling on one knee. Zack watched with a blank stare, and then glanced over at us with an "I'm-gonna-kill-you-guys-later" look. Then he centered himself, and did the deed.

The audience ate it up. He was so cute, and embarrassed, but did his best to remember the words and put on a great display for everyone. The place erupted in claps and cheers, and the waitress rewarded him with his super-duper-banana-chocolate-caramel-sundae. As he snaked his way past tables to get back to us, a few of the customers patted him on the back and told him he did a great job. I noticed a few girls who stared at him a bit longer than was necessary, and it made me a bit uneasy. *Hmmmm, jealousy maybe? That's a weird feeling.* As he sat back in his seat, he had a few choice words for us, but seemed to take it all in stride. Our sundaes arrived at the same time, and we all dug in, enjoying the rest of the show.

After Zack had been totally thrown to the wolves and we had devoured our sundaes, we were entertained with four Broadway Beltway show tunes from their candy striper waiters and waitresses. We sang along to songs from "Bye Bye Birdie" and "Oklahoma." The forty-five minute show was a blast, the ice cream was delicious, and we couldn't help but leave with a smile. It was the perfect place to go on a date. *Is that what this was? A date?*

As we shuffled out with the rest of the audience, Zack couldn't stop talking about the cheer he had done. He was bursting. Nick was quick enough with his cell phone to grab a photo and shared it with us. I think this was a highlight of Zack's vacation so far. He rode the whole way back to my house repeating the cheer, and we all couldn't help but laugh along with him as he did.

The streets of Cranberry Cove are pretty quiet at night. The occasional car will pass by, and you'll see some people walking along enjoying the ocean and bay breezes, but for the most part it's a very peaceful town at night. Our route home took us past the bayfront beach, and it was Nick who first pulled his bicycle into the parking lot and headed to the beach benches that overlooked the water. We followed behind, and parked our bikes as he did in the bike rack along the wooden rail fence separating the beach from the paved lot. Silently, we shed our flip flops and followed him over to the swing set that sat quietly overlooking the bay.

"Let's hang here a bit," Nick said, nodding towards the swings. "It's a nice night out."

"Sounds good to me," I added. One good thing about working at the Polar Palace is you don't have to get up early in the morning. Phoebe wandered quietly over to one of the swings and nestled herself into it. The rubber pad wrapped around her thighs and she began pushing herself into a twirl with her feet as she watched what was enfolding in front of her.

It seemed that she was trying that "hard-to-get" tactic. So far Nick didn't notice, but I was hoping that he would soon pick up on it. Zack walked up behind me and I felt his hand slip into mine.

"C'mon," he whispered into my ear. "Let's take a walk over there." He raised his chin in the direction of a turned-over rowboat, painted white with light blue trim and spelling out CRANBERRY COVE on the side. I followed eagerly, not sure why, but there was a "something unspoken" between Zack and me this night. I didn't know what it was, but I just felt as if he had put me under some sort of spell. I glanced over at the swings, and noticed that Nick had now slipped into the swing seat next to Phoebe, and I figured that it wouldn't be long before Phoebe would figure out where things were going between them.

Zack led me to a quiet spot on the other side of the rowboat. He guided me to sit on the sand, dropping my hand and then sitting down next to me. Then he grabbed my shoulders and pulled me over, gently, to nestle in between his legs. He pulled my back so I was leaning against his chest, his arm draped over my shoulder, my hands on his thighs. At first I tensed up, but I relaxed after I felt Zack take the pressure off, and I was somehow assured this wasn't going to become something I wasn't ready for. He was just cuddling, and we both stared out over the bay and watched the stars twinkle in the sky. The only sound was the lapping water against the shore, until Zack broke the silence.

"I'm really glad Nick asked me to come stay with him for a couple of weeks. I wasn't going to come, but Nick and I have become really good friends this past school year."

"I'm glad you came, too."

Silence. Then he spoke again. "Do you have a boyfriend… or anything?" His question was probing, but was spoken as if he wasn't sure if he really wanted to know the answer.

"No, no one special. How about you?" Now I wasn't sure if I wanted to know the answer.

"I had a girlfriend, but we broke up last month. She started acting weird, and then I found out she was cheating on me with a friend of mine." He sounded broken up about it, and I felt sorry for him. My poor Zack had his heart broken. I couldn't imagine anyone who would want to hurt this poor guy. He was cute, fun, and well, I'm sure he was a good kisser, too. I just imagined he would be.

"Sorry, Zack, I can't imagine how that would feel." It was all I could think of to say to him.

"Hey, whatever. It just wasn't meant to be." He shifted slightly and I leaned forward to allow him to reposition himself. Once settled, he pulled me back against him. I could feel myself getting very comfortable right now and it made me a bit uneasy. The warmth from his body was making me feel strange, and like an out-of-body experience, I felt my mind taking over and trying to convince me to start rubbing his leg or something. It took all the courage I had to will my hand not to move, not to stroke his leg. What was this going on inside me? It scared me a bit. And what was going on in his mind? Did he want something to happen here? Isn't that what boys do? Use charming tactics to get girls into a position where they can't escape? He was like a spider right now, and I was sitting right in the middle of his web. And I liked it. This wasn't good. I began to tense as my brain finally caught onto the reality of the situation. I pulled forward and spun around. It caught Zack off-guard. His face was surprised and he spoke out to me. "Hey, what's wrong? Did I hurt you?"

"No, I just, you know, I just . . . " I couldn't articulate what I was feeling. And frankly, I was embarrassed. Nothing happened, yet I just had that feeling that something might — something I wasn't ready for just yet. "I'm sorry, Zack. I'm just a little uncomfortable with this. You didn't do anything. You are a perfect gentleman." I smiled to soften the blow, as I certainly didn't want him to think that I wasn't interested in him in that way, but things were just kind of moving along a bit fast for me. He pulled his knees to his chest and wrapped his arms around them, grabbing his wrist with his other hand to keep them together.

"Sorry. Didn't mean to come on too strong. It's just that I like you, and wanted to spend some time with you — away from Nick and Phoebe."

"Speaking of Nick and Phoebe, what's the story with that?" I tried to get the subject off of us, and onto them in order to ease the awkwardness, and it seemed to help.

"Not sure. Nick likes her, but doesn't want to ruin the friendship. He's probably having that conversation with her right now."

We both glanced in the direction of the swing set, and could make out the two of them, still in the swings, talking quietly and using their feet to rock them back and forth as they spoke to each other. Phoebe's hands were grasped onto the chains of the swing, and Nick had his in his lap.

"I know. I got that impression. Phoebe's been trying to get his attention, but it hasn't worked. I think she knows, but isn't happy about it. She really likes him."

"Nick's a great guy. The girls at school all want a piece of him but he hasn't really been into anyone special yet. He likes hanging out with them, but that's all."

"I'm sure I'll be trying to cheer her up tonight after you guys leave. She's going to be crushed if this doesn't work out the way she's planning."

"Nick, too. He feels bad, but he's just not sure what to do. He doesn't know what will happen when they head home in the fall, and how that might change when he sees her again next summer."

We both sat watching them. Then I mustered the courage to figure out my own situation. "So, what is this, Zack, with us? Is this just a summer thing? A conquest to make your ex jealous? Or what? I'm not really interested in sporting a broken heart for the rest of the summer after you leave next week."

Zack looked at me with those big brown eyes. "I don't know. I like you. You're different from the girls at home. You're fun, and athletic, and pretty. And so, yeah, it's a summer thing. But maybe it's more than that. Who knows?" Well, you gotta give him credit for honesty. "What do you think this is?" he asked.

"I'm not sure, Zack. I'm still trying to figure that out."

PHHHTTTT! The watermelon seed flew through the air and stuck perfectly on the side of the shed. PHHHHTTTT! A second seed followed, but hit the shed and fell into the white daisies below. "Yessss! That's sixteen to two!" I shouted, the competitor in me showing itself once again while Phoebe mumbled some expletives under her breath and wiped her mouth with a swipe from the back of her hand.

"How do you do that? I can't ever get to them stick!" Phoebe cried out with a whine, and settled back against her chair to take another bite of her slice of watermelon. It was a sunny morning, and we hadn't spoken after Zack and I left her and Nick at the bay beach last night as they continued their talk, but Zack and I were ready to call it an evening. We had decided that we would see how our summer romance would develop, although cautiously, as I was still not looking forward to a broken heart that would inevitably appear sometime in mid-July when Zack headed back home to North Jersey. He was okay with taking it slow, and as we decided to sleep on it and headed back to the bikes, we left Nick and Phoebe on the swings to continue to work out their fate as we rode away. So, I was anxious to find out what the outcome was when I stopped by this morning and was greeted warmly by Phoebe's mom and some fresh sliced watermelon. Mrs. Pendleton was so sweet, and trusted me completely, so she never questioned when Phoebe was out late with me, or would call really late to say she was sleeping at my house. Since we lived on the same street, it gave Mrs. Pendleton peace of mind, I guess, that Phoebe would never be far away and into trouble. I'm glad about that. Trust is nice.

"So, about last night," I pressed. "What the heck happened? You two were so deep into conversation that we decided to not interrupt when we left. How did it work out?"

"He's so great, Casey, y'know? I really really like him. He's worried, though, about what might happen if we break up. He doesn't want to ruin a good thing. But he admitted he does like me, and wants to be with me this summer as something other than *friends*. I told him I do, too. So, we're going to just take it slow and see what happens."

"Hey! Me too! That's what Zack and I decided!" I got almost too excited on that revelation and it made Phoebe's eyes widen and light up.

"Jeez, I never saw you so excited before!" Phoebe giggled and then turned to the shed and leaning forward, spit a seed across the yard towards it. PHHHHTTTT! "Crap. Another miss."

PHHHTTTTT! "Yes! Perfect stick!" I puffed out my chest and raised my arms into a Rocky kind of pose.

"Doofus." Phoebe sunk back into her chair again. I looked at her and smiled.

"What do you want to do today? Beach? Let's just go relax and nap up there. I'm exhausted from last night. Too emotional for me. I'm not used to that stuff. And, I have to catch up on my reading! It's a great book, and the guy and girl are dating and..."

"Ugh! Enough! I don't want to hear! You want romance and drama? Look at us, Casey. This is a summer read in the making if I ever saw one!"

"Yeah, like anyone would ever read about US!" We both laughed out loud and went back to spitting our watermelon seeds against the shed.

The beach was perfect when we arrived. The bike rack wasn't filled yet, so we settled our front tires into the rack and headed to the entrance. We flicked off our flip flops and flashed our badges to the beach badge checker girl who was sitting under a very pink beach umbrella. Not a bad job for the summer, I thought, if you don't mind missing out on swimming. You did get a good view of the boardwalk, and did get to do some great people watching. If you were lucky enough to be assigned to guard the entrance across from the lifeguard headquarters, you got a good view of the Cranberry Cove hotties as they checked in for lunch breaks throughout the day. Phoebe and I love the beach, but we wouldn't want to be stuck sitting in a chair at the entrance. That's why we love working at the Polar Palace. A few hours at night is all we need to make some spending money, and still enjoy our days of free time on the beaches at the Cove.

Of course, the first thing I did as we walked onto the beach was scope out whether Jase was assigned to our swimming area. With twenty blocks of beach, and ten lifeguard stand stations along the oceanfront, there was always a chance he could be assigned anywhere in town. But luckily, because he had been on the squad the last few years, he'd been able to weasel in his own beach block assignment which is great for me. I was assured some eye candy in between my swims, and could glance up from my book to keep an eye on him as he disses the hot babes who all seemed to have an urgency to know what time it was, or what the water temperature was.

Today was no different. Before I even had my chair unfolded and my butt in it, I saw some tall drink-of-water with blonde flowing hair and a skimpy one-piece approach his stand. I quickly sat myself down and got ready for the show. She looked up, he looked down. She began to say something. The wind direction was from the west, so their conversation carried out over the water, not behind them to where I sat, so I was trying to imagine what they were saying. She talked, he responded, still looking down. I thought to myself that it was unusual, since he rarely let his gaze stay off the water for too long. He is usually very committed. I continued to watch as she threw her head back into a giggle, her hand slowly lifted until it was covering her mouth. She squinted up into the sun, raised her arm and placed her hand over her brow to shade her eyes from the glare. She tilted her head. The conversation continued. She reached up and handed him something. A little piece of paper. She gave a slight wave and walked away. He was still looking at her. And smiling. She looked back over her shoulder, waving again. He picked up his hand and waved, still holding that paper. Then he took the paper and stuck it into his backpack, hidden under his seat. *Hmmmm. I don't like this. I don't like this one bit.*

"Earth to Casey! What the heck are you doing? Didn't you hear anything I said?" Seemed she said that a lot to me when I was at the beach and Jase was working.

"Oh, sorry, I thought I saw a whale . . . " I turned my eyes to her, but then back to the lifeguard stand, and then over to the blanket and beach chair where the blonde had now positioned herself with her perfect long legs and blonde hair blowing in the breeze.

"Oh, not watching the girls talk to Jase again, are you? Doesn't that ever get old? What do you care who he checks out? He's gross, and believe me, you don't want him!" She sounded as if she was trying to convince me, almost disgusted that I was even interested. *Am I? Interested in him?* I let my mind ponder that as I settled back into my chair with my head back and closed my eyes to drift off.

16

My mouth was parched as I opened my eyes to view Phoebe napping soundly on the blanket sprawled out in front of me. I pulled my beach bag towards me and dug through to find my cell phone and glanced at the time. It was one o'clock and we'd been sleeping up here for almost two hours. My stomach was growling in protest, so I dug back into my bag to grab the pretzel rods and grapes I stashed there, along with my bottle of iced tea. While I nibbled and sipped, I let myself get lost in the scenery — the ocean waves filled with plenty of swimmers, the walkers and shell collectors carrying their finds in plastic buckets, and the boats far out in the water bobbing and drifting over the waves with fishing lines out in search of fluke. It was yet another perfect day at the beach, except for that display of the girl in the one-piece that was somehow nagging at me. I glanced over to where I saw her settling before my nap and noticed her chair was empty. I glanced over to the lifeguard stand. Only Jessica was up there. I then noticed that Jase was standing in front of the stand near the water's edge with the orange lifesaving float in his hand. He was talking to someone. I moved to my left to get a better view. GASP! It's her. He's talking to her!

The hair on the back of my neck stood up in an almost predatory reaction as I struggled to get a better view of what was happening before my very eyes. This one, this girl in the one-piece with the long blonde hair had obviously gotten his attention, and I was not enjoying this little show one bit.

"I'm going in," I stated out loud to Phoebe and anyone else in the vicinity, not knowing whether I meant into the water or to save Jase from the blonde-haired hussy. I trampled about three non-suspecting sunbathers as I trudged down towards the water's edge. I sidled up to Jase's left where I could get a good look at Blondie on his right.

"Hey, Jase, how's the water today?" I said to him, trying to sound sexy, but realizing I was using the same line as the other bimbos who approached him on the stand. I chastised myself, but kept my eyes on his while I did.

"Hey, Beach Girl, how are ya today? I haven't seen you riding any waves yet. You going in?" I noticed he glanced at my bathing suit — no doubt hoping that since I have my two-piece on, it would probably be a worth-while show for him to watch.

"Yeah, I'm thinking about heading in now. The waves look just about perfect." I glanced past him to see Blondie looking at me, no doubt trying to figure out the relationship, but also sizing up the competition as I had already done with her. Unfortunately, there was no competition. My athletic fourteen-year-old build was no match for her womanly shapely one, and I wasn't the only one who noticed that. I'm sure Jase knew who had won this competition. But, I figured Blondie couldn't compete with me as far as bodysurfing, and maybe Jase would find that more attractive than the two rather large eggplants that stared out at him from under Blondie's purple bathing suit.

I gave him a nod and headed into the surf, hearing his "good luck" that he'd thrown at me. I didn't look back, maybe because I didn't want to see them standing there, but instead headed out into the waves, doing my best dive under to get wet as a nice wave came at me head-on. I emerged, adjusted my top, and continued out past the breakers to the starting point. From that vantage point, I'd be able to assess what the situation was between Blondie and Jase.

The first two rollers came by, and the group of us who had gathered out in the water just floated passively over it. The third wave, though, had potential as it began to rear itself up and build in front of us. The six of us who had gathered in this spot, for obviously the same purpose, took note of its size and speed, and determined that this one could be it. We watched in awe as it took shape, and got excited as it continued to climb. This one was going to be a whopper. We all jockeyed for position, and once we felt the suction of the wave and it beginning to crest behind us, we all took off, swimming with it until it caught us up within its grasp and propelled us towards the beach.

I felt the familiar pull of the wave which told me that I had it. It carried me perfectly. I pulled my arms back with one more push and I glided over the wave, and in its fury, toward the beach. People in front of us scattered out of the way, some ducking underneath us, grabbing one breath that would last them until they could pop up the other side after it, and I passed over them. All of a sudden, something hit me. I was tossed and turned and gobbled up by the wave as it continued to drag me toward the shore. I heard the rush of water, felt the scraping of my skin on the bottom's tiny rocks and shells, and then — nothing.

One of the other bodysurfers tried to abandon the ride and turned into my path, not realizing I was there. He hit into me, and caused me to lose my balance, allowing the wave to swallow me up and toss me like an old sock in a washing machine. I tumbled all the way to the shallow water, legs flailing, arms trying to break my fall, but I couldn't stop my head from hitting the bottom. I blacked out, briefly.

Luckily, Jase was watching. He rushed over, leaving Blondie in mid-sentence, and ran into the shallows to drag me out. He also had the sense to pull down my bathing suit top quickly, to preserve my modesty. Grabbing both of my arms, he dragged me on my back up onto the shore line and dropped to his knees. He tapped my face with his palm to see if I was awake, and then thrust his lips upon mine. What he didn't know, was that I was breathing, and was now awake, and realized what he was doing. I guess he got caught up in the moment, but it seemed okay to me. I slowly opened my eyes as I heard him gasp, his lips still on mine. His eyes grew wide.

"Casey, are you okay?" I looked up to see his soft brown hair, his face close to mine, and the sun behind his head giving him a sort of halo around his entire body. The crowd that had gathered around us now collectively seemed to release their breath, as if they were holding it as this entire scene unfolded in front of them.

"Jase? Is that you?" I said breathily, although I knew it was, but somehow it just seemed the right thing to say at the time. "What happened?"

"What happened? I'll tell you what happened!" Phoebe's voice rang out from the crowd as everyone turned and gasped at her tone. "This doofus decided to turn right into you and knocked you clear across to the other beach! That's what happened!" She threw her hands up in a mock of disgust and then crossed them across her chest and shifted onto her other leg, shaking her head back and forth. "He could have killed you!"

Jase looked down at me again, taking his eyes off of Phoebe, no doubt hoping that no one would recognize them as siblings at the moment. "You think you can sit up? Here, I'll help you." He grasped one of my hands, and softly placed his other hand behind my shoulder and helped me sit up. I quickly remembered my two-piece, and my other hand instinctively went to my chest to make sure the girls were tucked away. "It's okay." He winked at me and spoke softly as if he knew what I was thinking. "I covered everything up for you." He smiled at me and I just looked into his eyes, some kind of weird unspoken connection, as if his kindness went beyond his job training for this type of situation. He really was worried about me.

"I, I think I can get up. Thanks, Jase." I smiled and steadied myself as I got up onto my feet. The crowd clapped, not for my performance, but for Jase's. I happened to notice Blondie with her mouth open, no doubt drooling over the hunky lifeguard who not only had her phone number stashed in his backpack, but had now saved someone during his shift. Jase reluctantly let go of my hand, but kept his hand on my back as he walked me up to my beach chair. He guided me into the seat and handed me my beach towel.

"You sure you're okay?" he asked, one hand on my knee now as he squatted down next to me.

"Yeah, I'm fine. My ego's bruised, though. Never had to get rescued before."

"I saw the whole thing. You had a great ride — the guy next to you ditched and ran right into you. It was his fault. And don't worry about it. The wipeout looked epic, too. Very graceful." He smirked and I knew he was only trying to make me feel better. *Could this guy be any cuter?* I smiled at him and wiped my face, but tried to remember the feel of Jase's lips on mine. "I gotta head back. I'll check on you later." And with that, he headed back over to the lifeguard stand, and back next to Blondie.

"What the hell, Casey? When are you going to switch into the one-piece already?!" I heard Phoebe admonish me sternly.

The local twitter site for Cranberry Cove erupted with photos that people took of the rescue. Jase was being hailed as a "hero lifeguard." The pictures were great, especially the one of Jase in the throes of giving me "mouth to mouth." I think I'll have that one printed out and framed! Luckily, I didn't see any which revealed my bathing suit top around my neck instead of where it was supposed to be.

I was tired and exhausted when we finally got home. Phoebe walked into my house with me and proceeded to tell my mother about what had happened, and asked her to convince me that one-piece bathing suits are my friend, and should be worn at all times. My mother was a trooper, and nothing I did surprised her, but after being assured I was unharmed and still her hero, she did agree with Phoebe. "Really, Casey, it's time — your base tan is there. Now just wear the one-piece. Save the bikini for non-swimming days, okay?" I couldn't say no to my mom. She really didn't meddle much in my business, and was always there when I needed her, so I took her words to heart and gave in.

"Alright already, you two. I'm moving to the one-piece." There were sighs of relief all around.

"Staying for dinner, Phoebe? Burgers on the grill tonight!" My mother loved burgers on the grill. We had them probably three times a week during the summer.

"Sure, sounds good. I'll call my mom." Phoebe headed to the couch to call her mom, and I headed into the kitchen.

"Nick has a friend down for a couple of weeks. Can I invite them over, too?"

Mom looked at me. "Of course, I love Nick. Haven't seen him yet this summer. How's he doing?"

"Great! Likes school. Misses being down here, though. I bet he'd move back here in a minute if he could."

"Divorce is rough on everyone, Casey. But sometimes it's a better alternative than living in a house with all kinds of screaming and yelling and resentment. People have to make decisions that are best for everyone, and unfortunately that sometimes means that families have to split up. But both Nick's mom and his dad love him. He knows that, doesn't he?"

"Yes, but as much as he loves his mom, I think he'd rather live here where he grew up."

"He'll graduate high school and go to college, and then he can live where he wants. Who knows? Maybe he'll end up back here one day. In the meantime, he can spend all summer here and you get to enjoy his company. Call him and tell him to come over for dinner, Casey."

"I will. His friend, Zack, he's, well . . . he's cute. You'll meet him and tell me what you think." I enjoyed that I could share stuff with my mom and not be embarrassed.

"Oh? Well, then by all means, call them. I'd like to see who has my daughter blushing!"

"Mom, it's not like that. At least I don't think it is!" We both giggled, and then Phoebe came into the kitchen to join us.

"What's so funny?" she asked, wanting to be included in our giggle fest.

"Casey likes Zack!" My mother sang out, trying to tickle me and tease me about it. "Casey's going to invite Nick and Zack for dinner, too."

Phoebe's eyes lit up. "Really? Cool! I'd like me some Nick for dessert!" My mother looked at Phoebe in surprise and then tried to tickle her as well. We all laughed at her outburst.

"Well, then by all means! Invite them over and let's see what the fuss is about here! I've obviously been left out of the loop! You girls both have crushes! Oh, to be young and silly again . . ." My mom's eyes were light with laughter and love, and she shook her head as she settled back into her kitchen routine of throwing together the burgers and shucking corn.

The sound of the stones in the driveway alerted us to our visitors' arrival, followed by the sound of rusted kickstands being extended and a rap on the front door. Phoebe opened the screen door and stepped aside as Nick and Zack greeted Phoebe and headed towards the kitchen. Nick walked right over to my mom and gave her a peck on the cheek and a quick hug greeting, while Zack was accosted by Sasha in the living room.

"Nick! How nice to see you! You look great!"

"Thanks! It's nice to be back. Thank you for inviting us to dinner. This is Zack." Nick put out his arm to present Zack, and we all turned, but saw no one. "Zack?" Nick called, walking back to the living room. As we followed, we saw Zack flat out on the floor with Sasha all over him, licking his face. Guess when he bent down to greet her, she pushed him over and wanted him to know how much she liked him.

"Sasha! Leave him alone!" My mom shouted as she tried to pull Sasha off him.

"Oh, that's okay," Zack said as he tried to lift himself off the ground. "I like dogs."

"Guess they like you, too, Zack." My mom threw her hand out to him to introduce herself. "Welcome to Cranberry Cove. How are you enjoying your vacation?"

"Great! I love it here! Not looking forward to it ending." He glanced over at me briefly. I'm sure I saw it. Maybe I just wished I had.

"Did you hear about the excitement on the beach, Nick? My brother had to rescue Casey today!" Nick turned his head quickly to Phoebe, and then to face me.

"What? What happened? Are you okay?"

"Yeah, I'm fine. A little mishap while bodysurfing."

"Oh, no. What bathing suit were you wearing?"

My mother let out a laugh. "Casey, don't you see now why you need to wear a one-piece?" She shook her head and headed back to the kitchen.

I motioned for the group to follow as I led them out through the back door and into the yard. We sat at the picnic table and caught up on the day's events. Phoebe was very animated as she relived every moment of the rescue, as well as my bathing suit malfunction. She took out her phone to show the pictures that we saved from the twitter feed and Nick and Zack huddled over her shoulder to see them. As she continued with her story, I excused myself to head back inside and help Mom with the dinner preparations. I also was anxious to hear her take on Zack.

"He's really cute, Case, and a gentleman! Nice manners and great eyes! A real catch!"

"That's my take as well, Mom. Too bad he'll be heading back north in another week."

"So what, Casey? Enjoy your time with him while he's here. What are you afraid of? This is what summer is all about." Mom had such a carefree way of looking at things. *Is she right?*

"We'll see, Mom. Phoebe is hoping to get her claws into Nick this summer. He's a bit reluctant, but she says it looks promising." I glanced out the kitchen window to the backyard to see them all perched around the picnic table deep in conversation. I turned back to my mom. "What can I bring out?" I grabbed the plate of molded burgers. Just then the back door opened, and Zack stepped in.

"Can I help with anything? I'm good at grilling. Can I start it up for you?"

"Thanks, Zack! That would be very nice! Mr. Whitman won't be home for a while yet, so I was going to try my hand at it, but I'm not very good at working the barbecue. So, yes, you are hired!"

"Great. I'll start it up." He grabbed the plate of raw burgers from my hand and looked me in the eyes. "Let me take that from you, Casey. You had a rough day. Go relax with Phoebe." He reached out and touched my cheek softly, took the plate from my hand, turned on his heel and headed out the back door. My mom's mouth was wide open, a half-shucked piece of corn in her hand.

"You can close your mouth now, Mom," I said as I grabbed her chin and pushed up.

"Wow, Casey. What manners. Don't throw him back — he's a keeper!" She winked as she said it.

Zack was right. He was a master griller. The burgers were fantastic, and he grilled the corn as well. The homemade potato salad, my mother's specialty, made for a perfect meal, as did the company and conversation.

"Will you be here for the Fourth of July fireworks, Zack?" My mother asked for which I was thankful as I hadn't yet had the conversation with Zack as to when he'd be leaving town.

"I leave on the sixth, so, yes; I will be here for fireworks. Nick said they are great. I'm looking forward to seeing them."

"Yes, they do a great job here on fireworks. They shoot them off over the bay and all the boats in the area sit in the Cove to watch them. Looks like the forecast is holding out as well so it should be perfect." The end of our block is across from the beach where the fireworks are set off, so all of the neighbors and my parents just bring their folding chairs to the end of the street and get a front-row view of the show. Since the street is closed off to traffic during the actual fireworks presentation, they really do end up with the best seat in the house. Unless, of course, you are sitting on one of the boats in the Cove.

Mom and I got up to start bringing in the leftovers and clear the table, and as soon as Zack jumped up, Mom was quick to sit him back down. "You did the cooking, we do the cleanup." That was all she said, and she meant it. He got the message.

"Thank you, Mrs. Whitman, dinner was great." Zack knew how to charm her. She caught the fever as well. We were all impressed.

Once inside, my mother couldn't stop talking about him. "Those eyes, Casey, and how he steals glances at you. So sweet. And manners! I like him. I really like him."

"Calm down, Mom, a bit too young for you!" I laughed, but I knew she was right. Why was I so reluctant to let this summer romance blossom? I must be crazy.

"Don't miss out on something because you fear getting hurt," she added. It sounded as if she was somehow speaking from her heart, maybe a regret she had at one time when she was young. "Just enjoy being young and experiencing young love. It's all good." She smiled at me and then dropped it. I think I knew what she was telling me to do.

Text between Nick and Casey:

Nick: Annual laser race on Friday. You in?

Casey: You need me? If so, YES!

Nick: Of course I need you. We win every year! You think I'd dump you now?

Casey: Thought maybe you'd ask Phoebe this year

Nick: What? You crazy? She can't sail! I want to WIN!

Casey: lol. In that case, I'm definitely in. Zack and Phoebe can cheer us on.

Nick: You break the news to her.

Casey: What are you nuts? That's your deal, buddy!

Nick: Ugh. Get ready for the aftermath.

Casey: Thanks for the warning.

I counted to twenty when the text from Phoebe came in.

Text between Phoebe and Casey:

Phoebe: You racing with Nick Friday?

Casey: Yes. You OK with that?

Phoebe: He didn't want me!

Casey: I'm sure he wants you, just not to race with.

Phoebe: You sure?

Casey: Yes. And while I'm on the boat, I'll ask him about you.

Phoebe: REALLY? Thanks, love! I owe you!

Casey: Just take care of Zack for me that morning. We'll all meet for lunch.

Phoebe: you got it!

Casey: You really aren't jealous of me and Nick, are you? Because its not like that.

Phoebe: I know. Just kidding. I'm good with it.

Casey: Cool. Work tonight? I'll pick you up.

Phoebe: okay. I'll be ready at 5:45.

Since Zack and Nick arrived, we'd been together at some point every day. Whether we were on the beach, or biking around, or hanging up in the center of town, we were inseparable. Zack and I were getting along great, and Phoebe and Nick were even making some progress. So far, nothing had gone further than some hand-holding. But something told me that tonight that was going to change. Phoebe had somehow put a time limit on how long it would be before Nick kissed her. That deadline somehow was tonight. So I was bracing myself for the fallout that would undoubtedly occur if the kiss didn't happen. Since we were working tonight, Phoebe arranged for Nick and Zack to pick us up after work, and we'd go to Benny's for a slice of pizza. Since we're done at 10:00 and Benny's closes at 11:00, we'd have time to grab a slice, and then take a stroll up to the beach. Phoebe had her heart set on the turned over lifeguard stand being the backdrop for her first kiss with Nick.

Our shift at the Palace went off without a hitch. We had the usual crowd, but nothing Phoebe and I couldn't handle. Everyone seemed happy, the music from the Crabby Tuna was wafting through the store and people were humming and singing along. One of the highlights of the night was when the entire place erupted into an impromptu sing along to "Sweet Caroline." It was priceless.

At 9:55 sharp, the ringing of the bell above the door signaled that our last customers had left. Phoebe ran over to bolt the door and change the OPEN sign to CLOSED, and then she turned to me.

"This is it! I'm so nervous! It's got to happen tonight!"

"Calm down, Phoebes. If it doesn't, don't be disappointed. It will happen when it's meant to be. Poor Nick. Don't scare him away!"

"Well, what about you and Zack? When are you two going to start making out?"

"Us? I have no idea! Don't worry about me, just concentrate on you."

"Can't you see that Zack wants you bad? Why aren't you more into this? He's really cute — not as cute as Nick — but cute. What's your problem?"

"I don't have a problem. I just don't feel like getting dumped in a week, that's all. Sue me." She was starting to get on my nerves. Actually, she wasn't getting on my nerves, but this whole what-is-going-on-with-me-and-Zack-thing was getting on my nerves. What's the worst that could happen? He's charming, good looking, polite, sweet, sexy... *ugh, did I just call him sexy?* He obviously likes me, and I like him, so what's a little kiss between friends? I'll make sure it doesn't go too far. I can surely do that, right?

Phoebe interrupted my thoughts. "C'mon, hurry up and restock! They're waiting outside!" I glanced out the front window of the shop. Sure enough, parked out on the bench were two of the cutest teens around, waiting for us to get off our shift. We finished up, and were out the door in five minutes.

"Hey, you girls hungry?"

"Sure, I can always eat a slice. You?" I caught Zack staring at me, and smiled a shy smile back. He winked. Ugh. Pressure is on.

We headed into Benny's and slid into a booth. Nick scooted next to Phoebe, and Zack next to me. The waitress strolled over and took our order for four slices and four cokes.

"So, you racing with Nick on Friday? Can't wait to see that! Nick says you guys always win."

"We sure do," I replied. "Nick is a great sailor, and I know how to follow instructions. I just do what he says when he says it, and somehow we end up crossing the finish line first."

"Zack and I will cheer you on from the Yacht Club and meet up with you for lunch afterwards." Phoebe had a bit of an attitude when she said it, but probably only because she wished she was able to sail with Nick instead of watching him from the sidelines.

"Well, be ready to take some pictures of us when we get that first place trophy, once again!" Nick pushed his chest out proudly. We'd won it two years straight, and he was pretty confident we would do it again.

Nick's job at the Cranberry Cove Yacht Club gave him access to so many people skilled in sailing. He'd often be asked to accompany them as first mate on trips when captains were taking guests out. Nick would basically sail the boat so that the captain could enjoy time with his guests, and from that Nick was able to pick up plenty of knowledge of handling a large variety of sailboats in all kinds of conditions.

Once during such a trip, a terrible summer squall popped up out of nowhere. It wasn't on radar, and it seemed to have formed just west of them as they were heading into the inlet from the ocean back into the bay. It's difficult enough to navigate either of the two inlets back into Barnegat Bay. They both are lined and marked only by large boulders and sand bars. They require maneuvering experience and good sense, and with a stiff wind from a squall that was gusty and accompanied by thunder and lightning, it was even more difficult to do. The quick change in winds caused the waves to become choppy and unnavigable. It caused the boat to pitch from side to side as the spray of waves came splashing over onto the deck. Nick was at the helm of the thirty-five foot sailboat when the squall hit, and instinctively he knew what to do. He was able to safely pull the boat into the waves, taking them head-on, almost effortlessly bringing the boat through the inlet channels and into the bay while the captain and his guests were hunkered safe and dry in the galley. Nick found a spot to wait out the squall, and then returned the boat and its passengers back to Cranberry Cove with no further surprises. Afterward, the captain of the boat recognized Nick at a Yacht Club dinner, telling everyone how Nick had saved his boat, and his guests, during that trip. Nick was thrilled, even more so by the $100 cash bonus Nick also received from that very grateful captain.

Nick's skills were far above any of the other summer employees who worked at the Yacht Club. When the boat races were posted on the bulletin board, other workers cringed when Nick's name appeared on the participation list. They knew he'd be real tough to beat. And with me next to him following his directions as he barked them out to me, it would be almost impossible. Nick and I worked like a well-oiled machine when we sailed. He had taught me so much over the past few years that I was almost confident enough to get a captain's license on my own.

We passed the time as we ate our pizza listening to Nick tell stories about past races, and about his dreams of one day joining a real sailing race team. We all agreed that one day we'd see him on one of those yachting magazine covers, holding up a huge trophy after winning a race in Australia or something.

The waitress came by to clear away our plates and glasses, so we guessed it was time to move on so Benny's could close up for the night as well. Outside, a slight breeze brought the smell of the saltwater right to us, and we followed that scent all the way up to the boardwalk. We parked at the bike rack, shed our flip flops, and headed through the cutout in the dune onto the beach. Another beautiful moon sat low over the water, lighting a pathway from the sandy beach right to it.

Nick was dragged by Phoebe immediately over to the flipped over lifeguard stand. He didn't have a chance to protest — she just grabbed his arm and led him there. Zack and I just watched, and then stood awkwardly together, not knowing what to do next. Thankfully, Zack was able to come up with something, or else we both probably would have been standing there for the next hour.

"Let's go take a walk. We'll come back in a little while to pick them up." Zack slipped his hand in mine, and I couldn't resist the cute but bashful smile that spread across his cheeks. I must have nodded, because he led me right down to the water's edge onto the firm sand where the waves rushed onto the shore. We began walking in the opposite direction of Phoebe and Nick, towards the bright lights that could be seen about a mile away from the amusement pier that sat in the next town to the south.

Quietly we strolled, our toes, heels, and ankles often being covered by the push of water from a wave as it crept up the shore, then retreated back into the surf while lapping as far up the sand as its momentum could take it. The water was chilled, but easy to get used to. Scattered shells lay in front of our path as we strolled hand-in-hand down the beach. "You're pretty quiet," I whispered to Zack, trying to break the silence and hoping that my thumping heart was being drowned out by the whooshing of the waves.

"So are you," he replied just as quietly, firming his grip and readjusting his fingers as if to make sure I was still attached to him. "Are you okay with me holding your hand like this?"

"Yes, it's nice." I had to be honest. It did feel nice. And the thumping of my heart was not uncomfortable, but exciting. My mother was right. Why was I so against this? It wasn't that bad at all. In fact, it was very enjoyable. We continued on our walk, Zack and I, not speaking out loud but somehow passing an unspoken comfort between us. The lights from the amusement pier began to get brighter as we walked. Or so I thought. The humming sound of an ATV was oddly placed into the background, drowning out the whooshing waves, and then two bright lights seemed to blind us as they turned into our path.

"Hey, Casey, how's it going?" It was Pauley. On patrol. And instead of his stealth police bicycle, he was straddling his hips and thighs over the seat of a four-wheeled all terrain rescue vehicle, one of the many gadgets used for patrolling the beach during day and night.

"Hey, Pauley. H-how are you? Nice night, huh?" I don't know why, but I reflexively pulled my hand out from Zack's and shoved both of them into my shorts pockets. "Zack and I — remember Zack? He and I were just heading over to the pier." I stammered, embarrassed at being caught on the beach at night holding hands with a guy. I don't know why, but somehow I instinctively was.

"Cool. Well, just be careful. You've got a great moon lighting the way for you tonight, so enjoy!" And with that, he sped off. I exhaled, not realizing I was holding my breath. Zack just stood there looking at me.

"You okay?" he asked.

"Yeah, I'm fine. All good." I smiled back at him, convincing . . . him? Or me? I'm not sure. But he was sure. So sure, he grasped my shoulders in his hands, and looked me in the eye. I saw his brown beauties drift from my eyes to my lips. His face inched closer. It was like a slow-motion movie, but I didn't have time to react. I was seeing it happen, but my mind couldn't process it. He moved closer, and his head tilted. The soft curls on his forehead shifted slightly as he angled his face to mine, closer . . . closer . . . I instinctively puckered up. He closed his eyes. I felt his lips connect with mine. Sparks, angels singing, fireworks, heat. Zack kissed me. Right there on the beach, in the moonlight, without asking, just latched on and kissed me. It was a soft, gentle kiss, but with enough electricity to light up that amusement pier. Neon flashers that were going off in my brain right then and as slowly as he touched my lips with his, he pulled away. He straightened his head and looked me in the eyes. A smile formed on those hot lips of his. He grabbed my hand, turned us around, and headed us back.

"C'mon. We'd better get back to Phoebe and Nick." And that was it. We walked back down the beach, back to where our bikes were parked in the rack. We never talked about what happened, not even to Nick and Phoebe, when we got back to the flipped over lifeguard stand. The four of us just headed back up to our bikes, and off we rode to head home for the night. As we rode in silence, my mind couldn't comprehend what I had felt. Surely I liked it, didn't I? I mean, there were fireworks and sparks and angels singing, right? That's good, right? So many thoughts were going through my head.

Later, as I crawled into bed, still wondering what had happened up on the beach, and trying to figure out how I felt about it, my phone vibrated indicating a text message had arrived. I looked at it in the dark. It was from Zack.

Text between Zack and Casey:

Zack: Had a great time tonight. Can't wait to see you tomorrow.

Well, I guess that explains it. It was great. Zack said so. *Wonder what greatness tomorrow will bring.*

I checked the calendar hanging on the refrigerator as I chowed down on my Frosted Flakes. Tomorrow is the race with Nick, and Fourth of July is two days after that. Two days after that, Zack will be leaving. Five more days of Zack and then my life will be back to where it was before, which was pretty darned uncomplicated. My thoughts were interrupted by Phoebe who had just arrived at my house with her beach bag. We would be heading up to meet Nick and Zack for some bodysurfing and boogie boarding, plans which were made last night between her and Nick while I was off gallivanting with Brown Eyes. She texted this morning when I was lying in bed still trying to figure out whether what had gone on last night was reality or a crazy dream. *It surely wasn't a nightmare.* Zack had kissed me. I think I liked it. It was a soft kiss, not a kiss you'd expect from a hormonal teenage boy, but one that a gentleman would give. It was a nice, romantic, soft, gentlemanly kiss. Like Zack. Yes, it was a Zack kiss. Would I let him do it again? Yes, I think I would. I convinced myself I would definitely let him do it again. If this was what a summer romance was, with soft kisses on a moonlit beach, then yes, I am definitely in! I will be with Zack. He will kiss me and I will like it. And I will live to tell about it. A nice summer romance that I can remember for the rest of my days. I had talked myself into it, and was ready for the next time he would kiss me. I sat back with a huge grin on my face for the first time since we left Benny's last night.

"What are you smiling about? I never got to talk to you last night. Did you make out with Zack last night on the beach?" Phoebe was busting to hear my story, but I think she really wanted to tell me her's first. So I asked.

"What about you? Did Nick get in under the deadline?" I raised my eyebrows up and down at her in rapid succession and made air quotes with my fingers to emphasize the word "deadline." She giggled.

"You doofus. Yes, we made out! It was great until Pauley rode up and interrupted us. Then we just hung out and talked until we saw you guys coming back up the beach."

"Oh, no! Did Pauley catch you, you know, all tangled up?"

"Well, we heard the beach buggy coming, so we were just sitting next to each other when he got to us, but we did kiss — a lot — and it was GREAT!" She sang the last part and her voice went up two octaves, hands in a little excited clap, followed by a squeal. She was definitely excited. "What about you guys?" She grabbed onto my arm as I was just shoving another spoonful of flakes into my mouth, and they ended up all over the floor. Luckily Sasha was there to lap them up.

"We . . . kissed," I answered matter-of-factly. "We also ran into Pauley, but we were just holding hands and walking. Pauley stopped to say hello, then drove off. Then Zack grabbed me, and just . . . well . . . kissed me."

"EEEEeeeeee! How exciting! So, how was it?"

"It was — nice, I guess. I don't know. I was kinda surprised by the whole thing. And it was weird — it seemed like the whole thing played out in slow motion." I twirled my spoon in the air while I spoke.

"EEEEeeeeee! A slow motion kiss! Like in the movies!"

"Well, not sure it was like the movies, but it was nice. He really is a gentleman. It was soft. His lips are soft. Really, really, soft." I found myself touching my own lips while I talked about it, as if trying to feel it again. "I don't know, I guess it's how it's supposed to feel. What do I know?"

"Nick was all slobbers and hands. Nothing like you describe. But mine were good. I think we've broken through the barrier, finally!" Phoebe did seem to be less tense this morning, like she had accomplished her goal and could now relax. I can't wait to hear Nick's side of it tomorrow, that's if he'll tell me while we're sailing.

The beach was packed when we arrived. The holiday weekend was approaching — one that is generally the busiest of the summer season. Looking across the sand at the many blankets and umbrellas and chairs staking out small claims to a coveted piece of the beach, we knew that this year was no exception. It wasn't difficult to spot Nick and Zack. They were the two crazy guys waving their arms wildly over their heads trying to get our attention.

"Let's go! We want to go in and we've been waiting for you!" Nick was screaming at us as we approached, dropping our bags and chairs down on their blanket. "The temperature is up to 72° today, and the waves are crashing!"

"Okay, I'm coming. Let me put down my gear and get my towel out. I'm happy to report that I'm wearing a one-piece, so there's one less thing to worry about today!"

"Thank God for that!" Phoebe whispered under her breath, but I still heard her. Zack was eyeing up the surf in anticipation. He'd been enjoying his romps in the sea, since the only natural body of water he'd been in was a cold lake with what he'd told us had turtles and snakes for swimming partners. The salt water had also done wonders for his skin, helping to bronze it with the help of the sun, and along with his blond-streaked hair he could easily have been mistaken for a Greek god, in my humble opinion. The tanned skin was also a great backdrop for his very white smile, which he had flashed at me, distracting me from getting my chair set up so I could hit the surf as well.

We ventured into the water, but not before I made a point to wander by way of the lifeguard stand where one Jase Hottie was once again on duty.

"Beach Girl!" He said as I strolled by. "Waves are kicking out there today. Make sure you use your blinker so we don't have any accidents out there." He winked. I smiled. She's there. Blondie. Stationed right next to the stand as well. I'm not sure how I felt about that.

"Will do — although it's the other guy who needs to use a turn signal. I take the waves straight into shore." I gave a hand movement that showed a smooth straight ride. And, as I flashed my best smile, Jase smiled back. I was hoping that Blondie had noticed.

The waves were great. I took about three straight into shore — no one was wiped out during my rides — and Zack was eager to learn the technique. Nick was teaching him how to spot the waves.

"I ran into some friends of mine this morning while we were waiting for you two," Nick said, "and they invited us to a party at their place Saturday night. His parents are going to Atlantic City, so he's throwing a bash. Sounds like it'll be fun."

"Cool! I'm in!" Zack said without taking his eyes off the horizon, still searching for any sign that another wave would soon be forming.

"Me, too!" Phoebe added, obviously wanting to be wherever Nick was planning to be.

"Ummmm, okay," I added, sounding hesitant, but not wanting to be a party pooper. I always hated going to house parties. Sometimes it would get rowdy, and I really wasn't into wrecking someone's beach house or watching someone else do it. Not cool.

"Oh, c'mon, Casey, don't be a spoiler. It will be fun. These guys are cool. I know one of them from home. It's his cousin's house. Nothing's going to happen."

"Alright! I'm in!" I needed to end the conversation because we all just caught sight of a huge wave and needed to get into position.

"I'm taking it!" Zack was looking so serious as he got into his stance, ready to take off into the wave. I decided to skip this one and watch. He looked too serious glancing from the wave, to the shore, looking to make sure no one was swimming in front of him so he could get a straight run in. Phoebe, of course, never rode the waves in. She was too busy looking for sharks or rogue kelp. She was only out here because Nick was. The wave lifted Zack and he swam and pushed, and off he went, looking pretty good until the wave crashed down and took him with it. He emerged looking pretty disheveled but unharmed. He caught our eye and swam back out, none too happy about the one that got away.

"Hey, it happens," I said as I patted him on the back. "There'll be another." And we resumed our positions with the old ladies floating in their nice flowered bathing caps.

The day of the race had arrived. Nick was texting me since 7:30 with local wind conditions and forecasts, already strategizing as to what we would need to do to win. I suited up in yet another one-piece, and hopped onto my rusty cruiser and pedaled down to the Yacht Club. Other sailors had already gathered and were working on preparing their laser sailboats for the race. Nick was there as well, checking his sails and untangling lines. It's always a pretty sight to see the small boats lined up along the shore ready to be launched, white sails against a light blue sky and darker blue water. Nick's laser is easy to spot because his sail has a huge grey seagull painted on it. The seagull is Cranberry Cove's symbol and it graces the water tower in town, greeting people as they arrive.

The forecast called for a chance of a shower, but there was no sign of any rain in sight right now. White puffy clouds drifted slowly in the distance, but above was nothing but sunshine. Nick saw me approaching and flashed a wave, looking a bit tense as he always did before a race.

"Hey, Nick, you ready to take another trophy today?"

"Hey, Case. Yeah, I'm ready. Looks like a lot of newbies will be racing today. Should be easy for us." This is the last year Nick would be in this racing category. Next year, he would move up into an older group, which skill wise was where he really belongs.

"Phoebe and Zack are coming at nine, and will meet us afterwards," I explained to Nick. "What do you need me to do to get ready?"

"Nothing. I'm all set. We need to shove off in about fifteen minutes, so relax until then." I nodded and looked around, eager to greet some of my other friends who also sail and would no doubt be in today's race. I spotted a few, and wandered over to pass the time and catch up on gossip.

Tweeeeettttt! The whistle from the Commodore, the head of the Yacht Club or who we would call "Mr. Burley from the Hardware Store," let everyone know that it was time to launch. Mr. Burley had been the Commodore at the Yacht Club for almost ten years. He's a big man with white hair and a white beard and looked like the fisherman in the fish stick commercial on TV. He'd been in town his whole life, and as a Navy veteran, he knew his stuff when it came to anything related to the water. His large presence could be intimidating to some, but not to me, and I made sure to go over to him and give him a big hug before the race. When he's not at the Yacht Club, you can always find Mr. Burley at the town's hardware store which his son now runs. Burley's Hardware has been in town for over seventy-five years; Mr. Burley's father opened it when he was young.

Nick waited for me to settle into the laser before he pushed it into the water and hopped in himself. With about twenty boats participating in our particular race today, maneuvering out into the open bay would be a challenge, but Nick was able to weave through the other boats and lead the pack as we headed out to the large orange buoys that were in place just for this event. The wind seemed perfect for sailing and would be an asset for all of the sailors going through the course set out for us.

Sailing is fun. It's a simple concept — you harness the power of the wind to propel your boat forward. The trick is to understand how to adjust your sails to take maximum advantage of the wind. If you can master that, you can move in any direction regardless of how the wind is blowing. A major difference between a sailboat and a boat with a motor is that while a motor boat can go in a straight line regardless of wind, a sailboat will have to tack back and forth, adjusting its sails in order to allow the wind to push it along. Sailing is for people who aren't in a rush as sometimes the wind may die out and you would be drifting waiting for another puff to come through to push you again. In that way, it is very relaxing. But in a race, you are never relaxed. The race is a test of skill and knowing how to position your sail in just the right way to give you speed, especially when you enter a turn and need to spin the boat to head into another direction. Nick is great at timing his turns perfectly and making quick sail adjustments. He has a shelf full of trophies to prove it.

As soon as we moved into starting position, Nick turned to me and barked out the first of many orders he'd throw at me throughout the race. We went from friends to Captain and Mate, and I understood my role. I was there to take orders and do what he would ask of me, and since we'd done it many times before, I knew that our fun playful banter would have to be set aside for the next twenty minutes. I remembered the first time I had sailed with Nick and he tried to explain the many nautical terms to me. At first I had no idea what he had meant, but eventually the words made complete sense to me. Now when he tells me he's going to "starboard tack to the reach" and to "adjust the mainsail to the aft," I actually know what he's talking about.

"All set, Casey? Let's bring that trophy home!"

"Aye, Captain! As you say!" I loved how Nick was so competitive when it came to sailing. He made it look so easy, too. I'm grateful that he asks me along for these races.

"HOOOONK!" What sounded like a goose with a bad cold was actually the horn to start the race. Nick pulled the sheet (the line) to adjust the mainsail and we bucked into a forward movement. The boom (the tube that holds the bottom of the sail in place) was pulled to the starboard (right) side of the boat and the wind puffed the sail out as we forged ahead of the pack. Nick's movements were quick and tidy. I paid close attention to what was going on as I tried to anticipate his next move.

We leaned out the side of the boat as it tilted from the wind pushing against the mainsail. If you don't do this, you'll capsize the boat, which happened often when he was first teaching me. Nick held onto the sheet and let it out ever so slightly to adjust the sail again as we approached the first buoy. We'd be making a turn, and it would require a quick adjustment of the sail and ourselves once he tacked into it.

The rest of the sailors were just behind us, and one boat was next to us. It would require our turn to be tight, so Nick waited until we were just at the buoy to yell "Tack!" and we both ducked as he pushed the tiller, which controlled the rudder, and put us into a turn. At the same time, the boom swung around and over us as we ducked and moved to the other side of the boat. The boat tilted again, and we positioned ourselves on the other side as Nick pulled at the sheet and once again the mainsail puffed out as it caught the wind. It was a successful maneuver, and it gave us a bit of an edge on the boat that was next to us, as they were falling a bit behind. Nick looked back at them and then looked ahead and smiled, and I knew what he was thinking. They were no match for us right now.

The course required us to make three full laps around it, and all of the tacks we made on our first two laps went smoothly. The closest boat to us was still just a bit behind us, but they were still a tough competitor. They hadn't gotten closer, but they hadn't lost any ground either. It would prove to be a tough race for sure, and Nick continued to bark out orders to me and I continued to follow them without hesitation.

On the last lap, however, Nick noticed that the other boat had come very close to us, just a few feet off our stern. It would require Nick to be quick on our next tack, or else the other boat might run into us. He told me to get ready, and I braced for the boom to begin to move towards me as I held the sheet of the sail.

"Tack!" Nick yelled, and I pulled and ducked, as he threw over the tiller and the rudder swung across the stern of the boat causing us to turn. But the boat behind us turned too soon and clipped the portside of our boat. I held on as the boats bumped, but the boom on the other boat swung over and clipped one of its sailors in the head, and she fell overboard into the water. Without even thinking, Nick dropped the tiller and jumped in after her. Although she was wearing a life jacket, she was face down and unconscious, afloat in the water.

The other boats were still involved in the race and were still well behind us, and no one on those boats noticed what was going on. The other member of the boat following us noticed that his mate had hit the water, and yelled out, "Man overboard!" I had to act quickly in order to keep our boat from tipping, so I let out the sheet and allowed the mainsail to fluff. The boom rolled back and forth as the boat rocked on the waves, and I searched the water frantically to see whether Nick had reached the distressed sailor.

"Casey! Pull the boat around!" Nick now had his arm around the girl's neck, in a lifeguard hold, as she was floating on her back, and he'd already begun paddling his way back to the boat. By the time he reached us, there was a stream of other boats flying past us, continuing on with the race. I reached over the port side of the boat and grasped under her arms. With all my might, I dragged her onto the deck of the laser. Nick hoisted himself over the stern and pulled off his lifejacket. He positioned himself over her, leaned close to her mouth and checked for breathing. Carefully lifting her neck so her head tilted back, he pinched her nose with the fingers of his other hand and began mouth-to-mouth resuscitation. Slowly, carefully, and seemingly on autopilot, he continued the breathing and chest compressions until the girl began to cough and turn her head to spit out water. He lifted her up to a sitting position, and spoke to her, telling her that everything would be okay. She seemed in a daze, but then her eyes met his. She was shaking, obviously scared, but Nick's soft voice was soothing to her, and she grasped his arm as if she was trying to understand what had just happened. I watched as Nick pushed the hair off her face and held her hand, telling her to breathe and relax. Color returned to her cheeks. She looked at him and smiled.

Nick instructed me to pull the sheet to bring the boat around and head back into shore. With the race just about over, and the other boats now on the other side of the course, we headed towards the Yacht Club with our precious cargo. The other boat from which she fell was close by, trying to see if she was okay. Nick gave him a wave and motioned to him that we were going in, with a thumbs up which the other guy obviously deciphered as a good sign and I noticed his shoulders drop, seemingly to let out a sigh of relief. I took the tiller and positioned the boat for a ride in, while Nick sat on the deck with the girl who was still recovering from that very scary ordeal.

I heard Nick speaking to her softly, and asking her name and asking if she had remembered what happened. She said her name was Cate. She was very grateful to Nick for jumping in after her, and told him so. He seemed almost embarrassed at the praise she gave him, his shy smile obviously melting her heart just a bit. I was happy for her that Nick was around to see what happened. If not, she may have drowned.

As we reached the beach, the Commodore was there to meet us. One of the race supervisors had called ahead after realizing what had happened, and Mr. Burley raced into the shallow water in his khaki pants and boat shoes to check on us. He informed us that an ambulance had been called and had just arrived, and he thanked Nick profusely for his quick action to help her. Zack and Phoebe were on the beach, and watched as Nick helped the girl to her feet and out of the laser, into the hands of the Cranberry Cove Emergency Response Team who were already there with a stretcher, checking her pulse and shining a little flashlight into her eyes.

"Whoa, Nick. What a save!" Zack slapped Nick on the shoulder and grabbed on, giving him a side hug. "You Da Man!"

"You should have seen him! He never hesitated! Just jumped right in . . . like . . . like . . . Superman!" I shouted, obviously very proud of my friend.

"Superman, huh?" Nick asked, almost in a whisper. He turned to Mr. Burley. "May I ride with her? To the hospital? Her parents aren't here." Mr. Burley looked over at the EMT tending to Cate. He shrugged in agreement, and Nick headed off as they wheeled her over to the waiting ambulance. We all watched as they lifted the stretcher into the back, followed by Nick. The door closed and off they drove.

"Wow! That was crazy! Casey, tell us what happened! Were you scared?" Zack was so amazed by what he just witnessed and wanted every detail.

"It happened so fast. We were heading into a curve, and Nick saw her fall off her boat and he never hesitated, just jumped in. It was... surreal! He swam her back to the boat, we lifted her on, and Nick gave her mouth-to-mouth because she wasn't breathing. After a few breaths, she coughed up some water and then she seemed okay. Nick never panicked throughout the whole thing. He just — did it. It was like watching a movie or something. He's really a hero."

Phoebe was really quiet throughout this whole time, just listening. I didn't realize it until I heard her speak. "Why did he go with her in the ambulance? Does he know her?"

"No, he didn't know who she was. He was asking her questions on the boat I think just to calm her down. She said her name was Cate. She thanked him a million times. He just held her hand until we got . . ." I stopped. I didn't realize it, but the details of my story were like a knife plunging into Phoebe's heart. I looked at her. Her eyes were tearing up, and her lip was trembling. Was she — jealous? Hurt? Surely she couldn't be angry at Nick for wanting to make sure this poor girl was safe. They both just went through a very terrifying ordeal — Cate almost drowning, and Nick saving her life.

"Phoebes, are you okay? Nick just wanted to make sure she was okay — he saved her life out there. Are you upset about that?"

"I don't see why he had to go with her! He didn't even say goodbye to us! He didn't even look at me! He . . ." and she burst into tears. Zack and I stood there in shock and then he put his arm around her.

"Hey, Phoebes, don't cry. Nick's still running on adrenaline and wants to be sure she's okay. He's not dumping any of us. C'mon, let's go get something to eat inside. I'm sure he'll be back soon." We headed up to the porch and grabbed a table. All around us people were talking about the rescue and Nick, and how a great tragedy was avoided today because of Nick's quick-thinking actions. I was proud of Nick, too, and loved listening how everyone talked about him being a hero. *Way to go, Nick!*

When I got home, I told my mom about what happened. She said she'd already heard from Pauley. He was on duty when the call came in about a possible missing boater, and how he found out that it was Nick and me that played a part in the rescue.

"Oh, Honey, I'm so proud of you two for not panicking and knowing what to do in that emergency! From what Pauley said, Nick saved that girl's life! And you were right there at the controls to get them both in safely. I'm so proud of you!"

"Well, Phoebe isn't. She is so mad at Nick for going in the ambulance with that girl, Cate, instead of staying with us."

"Oh, that can't be true. Phoebe wouldn't be jealous of that, would she? Nick wanted to make sure she was okay. Imagine how scared he must have been, thinking that girl could have died if he wasn't able to revive her. And he trusted you to get the boat back in while he was helping her. You both are heroes!"

"No, not me. I was just following Captain's orders. Nick is the man of the hour, not me." I couldn't stop smiling when I thought of him. I really am proud of my friend.

"Have you heard from him?"

"No, but I'm going to text him to see how he's doing." I pulled out my phone and typed.

Text between Casey and Nick:

Casey: Nick! Where are you? Still at hosp?

Nick: Yea, Cate still getting checked. Called her parents, and they are on their way.

Casey: How much longer?

Nick: Not sure. Maybe an hour?

Casey: You were great today.

Nick: You too.

Casey: Thanks. See you later?

Nick: Yea. Where's Zack?

Casey: Went home. Took Phoebe.

Nick: Crap! Phoebe.

Casey: Yea. You need to text her.

Nick: Okay. See ya later

Casey: K

Nick: We didn't win.

Casey: Lol. No, but that's okay!

Nick: Yea.

I headed into my bedroom and plopped onto my bed. Sasha followed me, jumping up and cuddling into a ball behind my knees. I rested my head on my pillow and continued to replay the day's events in my head. Looking back, I was really proud of how I handled the boat while Nick was in the water, and afterwards getting us all back to shore. A huge smile erupted on my face as I closed my eyes and let sleep take me over.

I awoke a few hours later and noticed the sun had that late afternoon hue to it as it peeked through my bedroom window. It was sitting low in the sky, so it must have been close to four o'clock. I reached for my phone and noticed two missed calls and a few frantic texts from Phoebe stating that Nick still hadn't been in touch with her. I texted her back.

Text between Casey and Phoebe

Casey: Phoebes, just woke up. Crashed after I got home.
Phoebe: Have you heard from Nick?
Casey: Yea, I texted him …

I erased that line. Started again.

Casey: No, not since the hospital. He's probably exhausted and napping.
Phoebe: What the heck? He can't return one text?
Casey: Where's Zack?
Phoebe: Went back to Nick's house.
Casey: I'll text Zack to see what he knows.
Phoebe: TEXT ME BACK!!

Okay, I could see now that Phoebe was one step away from doing something stupid if I wasn't able to find out where Nick was. I texted Zack.

Text between Casey and Zack:

Casey: Hey Zack, any word from Nick? How's Cate?
Zack: Cate's good. Nick is still there.
Casey: Really? Did her parents show?
Zack: Yea. Nick wanted to stay a while.
Casey: ?
Zack: Yea, I know. Did you talk to Phoebe?
Casey: She's frantic.
Zack: Yea, she was when I took her home. Wanna hang out tonight?
Casey: Sure. What do you want to do?
Zack: Mini golf?
Casey: Fun! What time?
Zack: I'll come get you. Around 7?
Casey: Working til 10.
Zack: Can we go after?
Casey: Yes! Open until midnight!
Zack: It's a date!
Casey: Okay. What about Nick and Phoebe?
Zack: Hopefully he'll text me back before then.
Casey: See you at 10 at the Palace.

I wasn't sure what to tell Phoebe. I didn't think telling her that Nick was still at the hospital would be a good thing. So I just texted Phoebe and told her that I couldn't get in touch with Zack either. I told her I'd try again in a bit. She seemed okay with that, and I figured I'd try one more time to reach Nick. So, I texted.

Text between Casey and Nick:

Casey: Nick! What's up? You still at hospital?

Nick: Hey - yea, coming home soon.

Casey: She okay?

Nick: Yea, they're going to keep her overnight to check on her.

Casey: Wanna mini golf with us tonight?

Nick: Not really. I'm beat.

Casey: Do me a favor?

Nick: What?

Casey: PLEASE TEXT PHOEBE!

Nick: You yelling at me? lol

Casey: YES! please?

Nick: Okay, I'll do it now. My dad's on his way to get me.

Casey: Okay. See you tomorrow.

I waited a few minutes before texting Phoebe back, in hopes that Nick would have contacted her and she'd be a bit less stressed. We had to be at work at 6 pm, and I anticipated a very long night of moping and tears over this whole situation, even though there probably wasn't even a real situation at all. In Phoebe's mind, Nick abandoned her, and he needed to fix that so I could get through tonight's shift without shoving her in the freezer at the Palace. It wasn't long before Phoebe texted me, saying that Nick was on his way home and wanted to play mini golf tonight after our shift. With a sigh of relief, I sunk back into my pillow, thankful that things would now hopefully get back to some semblance of normalcy. *What a day!*

The Friday night of the Fourth of July weekend was always one of the busiest days in town. The island seemed to explode with people — those who had summer homes, those who rented summer homes, and those who visited people who owned or rented summer homes. The streets were packed with cars, bikes and people walking around. There was always an electricity in the air as everyone was celebrating a long holiday weekend, great beach weather, and sporting some great sunburn. Inside the Palace, we were packed from the minute we arrived, until we were ready to close. The time flew by quickly, and that was good. Phoebe had almost no down time during which to grill me about Nick or Cate or anything else. I was spared the routine of having to cheer her up, and I had to admit that I had things on my mind tonight as well, namely my "date" with Zack to play some mini golf.

At 9:55, the bells above the door jingled as Nick and Zack arrived. It would still be a while before we could close, as the last customers were still working on their sundaes and cones. Phoebe went over to lock the entrance door and change the sign to CLOSED, and we proceeded to clean up behind the counter, and refill the supplies we'd used. Once the customers were done, we would be able to head over to play golf. Luckily, one older gentleman at a table noticed what we were doing, and announced to his party of five that "These girls need to close up, so we better hit the road." I gave him a grateful smile, and told him to take his time, but he glanced over at Nick and Zack with a wink, and then shuffled his group to the door. The other tables took note and also began to leave, waving goodbye and throwing thank-you's over their shoulders as they retreated. Before we knew it, the place was empty, and we were ready to go.

Zack and I began to head outside to the bike rack, and I noticed that Nick and Phoebe stayed behind inside the shop for a few minutes. I imagined Nick wanted to talk to Phoebe and explain, you know, clear the air a bit before we rode to the mini golf course. Zack and I grabbed our bikes and watched through the window as Nick was talking to Phoebe, and we watched Phoebe's reaction as she became a bit animated in her responses. They both seemed calm, and before long they were wrapped around each other in a hug, Nick's face looking relieved. As Phoebe stepped out, locking the door behind her, I saw her wipe her eyes discreetly with the back of her hand before the keys went into her pocket. Soon after, we were all headed down to the south end of town to the mini golf-and-arcade place known as Salty Sam's.

Salty Sam's is a great place. The arcade is big, and is housed in a building that has no windows, just garage doors. When the arcade was open, the doors were raised to make the place look like it had no outside walls. The pinball machines, video games and skeeball games were packed side by side inside, and the flashing lights looked as though there was an electrical storm going on inside the building. The lights, along with the sounds of pings, explosions, whistles and bells from the games were an overload to your senses. A trained ear could tell what games were being played, but to an untrained rookie it just sounded like noise.

The golf course is set right next to the arcade building. A huge statue of Salty Sam holding a golf club stands in the middle of the course and his legs are actually part of one of the obstacles for the twelfth hole. In the winter, Sam is stored away so he doesn't get damaged by the snow, wind and ice, but once he emerges in spring the locals all know that summer can't be far behind. The tourists see Sam as a landmark, and many will stop and take pictures of themselves with Sam in the background.

While I'm good at many things that make up the Jersey Shore, mini golf is not one of them. I just don't have the coordination to putt that little colored golf ball through the windmill arms, or over the little hill, or under the bridge without it ending up three holes down in the middle of someone else's game. I imagine I'm not alone. That is probably why everyone gets a different colored ball so that they can be identified and retrieved at other spots around the course.

Zack stepped up and paid the lady in the booth for our game and was handed a little paper scorecard and a tiny pencil. We went over to pick out our putters, and he handed me a pink ball. His was green. We stepped aside and waited for Phoebe and Nick to meet us and then we headed to the first green. Nick was playing a blue ball and Phoebe had yellow. I know, because she screamed out, "Oooh, yellow's my favorite color!" to the lady when she placed them onto the counter. So now everyone at Salty Sam's was also aware that Phoebe's favorite color was yellow. We shook our heads and headed over to the starting tee.

At the first hole there was big crab. You had to hit the ball into the crab's open mouth, and it was supposed to emerge out one of his many legs. Hopefully, it came out of the leg that would aim it right near the hole. It was a par three, so even the guy that designed the course was thinking that this would be pretty easy. Zack waved his arm toward the tee, and with a gallant bow he uttered, "After you, my lady."

"Well, thank you, kind sir." I played along with his banter, and added, "'Tis a gentlemanly gesture, and I do thank you. Now please, step aside, or you may be beheaded as I swing my iron rod." He giggled and stepped back, and I took great care to position my pretty pink golf ball onto the first tee and center myself, ready to putt. I first looked at my target — the crab's mouth. It was only a few feet away and surely I could aim the ball close enough to get it inside without much effort. I looked down at the ball, pulled my club back and carefully tapped the ball, making sure to follow through on my swing like they do on The Golf Channel. The ball moved forward, and stopped before it even reached the crab's mouth.

"That's one stroke!" yelled Phoebe. I turned and gave her a dirty look. She knew this wasn't my sport and she was ready to take advantage of me. Well, I was not going to give her the satisfaction.

"Just hit it from there," Zack whispered to me, pointing at the mouth of the crab. "You can do it." I saw him stifling a smile as he did.

"Hey, I got this." I confidently stepped back up to the ball, assessed my target which was now just inches away, and tapped. The ball moved slightly off to the side, and missed the crab's mouth.

"That's two!" Phoebe was really excited now. I gave her another dirty look, and turned back to the ball.

"Just relax, Casey, it's just you, and the ball. Ignore everyone else," Zack whispered, his formerly hidden smile now making an appearance broadly across his face. Oh, they were all enjoying this, and we were only on the first hole. I could see that this was going to be a very long night.

The rules of the game state that after three tries, you can bypass the obstacle, in this case it's the crab, and toss your ball over to the other side. I opted to do that, as now there was a long line of people behind us grumbling about how they'd be able to catch the sunrise if we didn't hurry up and move the game along. Zack, Nick and Phoebe had no trouble hitting the mark and each were rewarded with their colored golf balls settling nicely in front of the hole to the crab's rear. They were also rewarded with low scores on that round. We moved on to the next putting area which featured two rolling hills. If you got the ball to roll over each hill, then you were pretty much set on getting it into the hole. The goal was to do it on only two strokes, so this one should have been a breeze.

"You're up, Casey. Just take your time and put some oomph into this one in order to get the ball over both humps." Zack was hopeful that this hole would be a bit easier for me. I think he was sensing that I'm not comfortable with this game at all. Phoebe and Nick were snickering, knowing that it was killing me that I couldn't play well. Somehow, mini golf is my nemesis, like kryptonite to Superman. It showed my weakness, which I really hated.

"Okay, this is when I turn it around," I told them all. "I've got this one!" I set my pink ball down and, remembering Zack's suggestion to give it some oomph, I centered myself, pulled back the putter, and gave it a good shot. Not only did the ball roll over the two humps without any effort, it continued to roll through two other greens and into the pond on Hole #6. I watched as a little boy bent over, reached into the pond, and pulled it out. Water ran down his arm as he yelled over in our direction, "Does this ball belong to anyone? It almost hit my mom!" I looked over at Phoebe as she was ready to point out that I'd just used up another stroke and gave her the don't-even-try-it look. She pulled in her lips and made the "zipped" sign across her mouth. I then trudged over and retrieved my ball from the boy, thanked him and apologized to his mother.

The game continued on and I was now losing by about twenty strokes. But we were all having some fun and I found I was enjoying being in Zack's company. I watched him at each hole as he prepared to putt and I took note of his features: great profile, muscular build, warm and inviting eyes, a smile to die for. I found myself fantasizing about what it would be like to be held in his arms, in one of those great hugs that I read about in my beach novels. I mean, would it be so bad to make out with this guy?

That's what teens do, right? Harmless kissing and hugging? And what can happen? He's leaving in a few days, so what's the worst thing? I miss him? At least then when I read my beach novels I'll be able to relate to the love scenes because I'll have already experienced it, right? As I'm deep in thought about this, I saw Zack look over to me as if he could read my mind. He gave me a slow smile and a wink (*a wink!*) and I quickly turned my eyes away. Does he know what I'm thinking? *Oh boy.*

"Last hole!" Phoebe yelled out. "If you get a hole-in-one, you win a free game!" Her enthusiasm was proof to her happiness being at Nick's side throughout the course. I was happy for her, and for him, that they'd talked through Phoebe's insecurity about his feelings for her. Obviously, he was happy with the way things were working out between them.

"Casey, you can redeem yourself on this hole. If you can get a hole-in-one, maybe we can find a way to celebrate," Zack whispered to me, so only I could hear it. I froze. But somewhere out of who-knows-where, words formed on my tongue, and leaked out of my mouth.

"You're on." I turned and smiled, then placed my ball on the tee and centered myself once again. Pulling back my putter, I looked at my target, and tapped. The ball rolled down the green and plopped right into the cup.

"You did it!" screamed Phoebe and she started to do some type of very embarrassing happy dance.

"Yes, I did." I whispered to myself, and glanced at Zack — showing the surprise on my own face at what had just occurred.

"Well, a celebration seems to be in order," he whispered in my ear as he brushed past me to take his turn.

After a quick refreshment from the snack stand, and a calculation of final scores, we determined that Zack was tonight's winner, followed by

Nick, then Phoebe, and far behind, me. It was okay, though, because I knew that Zack's promise would be the prize I would be looking forward to, and it would be a hundred times better than the free game I'd won. I gave my free game coupon to Nick to give as a prize to one of his students at the Yacht Club.

"It's getting late, we better get out of here and head home," Nick mumbled, checking his watch. Tomorrow was Saturday and he'd have to give some lessons in the morning.

"I'm going to visit my grandmother in the morning with my mom, so are we still on for that party tomorrow night? I'll be back in time for work, and then we can head over afterwards." Phoebe was so looking forward to going to the party with Nick, and looked over at him just to be sure they were still going to the party together.

"Yeah, we're still going. Pick you up from work and then we'll ride over. Okay, Phoebes?"

"Perfect."

"Why don't you and Phoebe head out. I want to talk to Casey for a few minutes. I'll meet you home, okay, Nick?" I froze and looked across the table to Phoebe, who couldn't hide the smirk that appeared on her face, accompanied by the big eyes and raised eyebrows that stared back at me.

"Oh, ah . . . yeah, that's fine. C'mon, Phoebes, let's get you home. See you at home, Zack." Nick glanced at Zack, and then me, wondering what was up. Hey, I was wondering as well. This must be part of that celebration that he promised. I waved at Phoebe and Nick as they headed hand-in-hand to the bike rack. I watched as they rode off. Once they were out of sight, Zack took hold of my hands in his as he leaned across the table.

"You up for a walk on the beach? I believe I owe you a celebration. What do you say, a moonlight stroll?"

"Ummm . . . okay." My feet seemed to be plastered to the floor under the wooden picnic table — I managed to get them out with the help of Zack holding my hand and directing me to the sidewalk leading up to the beach.

"Just a quick walk," he said, as if reading my mind again as I was trying to decipher exactly what this celebration might entail. Anxiousness and excitement together made me lightheaded, but in a good way. I was really enjoying this adventure and wasn't worried at all that Zack wouldn't be a gentleman. In fact, I soon found myself walking faster than he was, and was almost pulling him along up the wooden pathway. As we neared the opening in the dunes, we were greeted by a breathtaking view of the nighttime beach — illuminated by a beautiful moon. The shimmer of light on the waves as they pushed to shore sparkled like silver beads. The sand was flattened by the movement of the water as it rushed back to the sea, only to be covered by the next wave as the rhythm repeated, like background music being played by Mother Nature only for us. I followed his lead as he kicked off his flip flops by the dune, and without hesitation Zack led the way down to the water's edge.

No words were needed right now. He led and I followed. We walked with our toes in the sand and water at a slow pace, enjoying the solemn mood, just staring at the ground in front of us. "You know I'm leaving in a few days."

"I know."

"I'm really going to miss you."

"Me, too. I wish you were going to be staying longer."

"Yeah, me, too. But I gotta head back north. I'm going to visit my mom's relatives in upstate New York and spend two weeks there. There's no ocean, like this," he pointed to the water as he looked out into the horizon, then glanced back to the sand below as we walked, "but there's a lake. We do a lot of fishing there."

"Do you like it there?"

"It's nice. I never went to the beach when I was young, only up there, so that's all I knew. This is really nice, too. I like being at the beach. It's . . . different."

"I know. It's like a fairy-tale place, right? People always say that. There is no place in the world like the Jersey Shore, from what people say. I guess that's why people come back every year. It's just special."

"You're lucky to live here all year round. Most people only get a week or two to enjoy it."

"I am lucky."

"And I'm lucky, too. Lucky to have met you." And with that, he stopped and spun me around, wrapping his arms around me. Face to face, he looked into my eyes as if searching for something — an answer? My approval? I saw his eyes dart from one to the other of mine. And then he slowly brought one hand up towards my face, and with his finger he pushed my chin up from below until my head was tilted up and angled into his, and his gaze shifted to my lips. Then he closed his eyes and kissed me. Slow. Soft. I reached up and placed my hands on his forearms and held him there. It was a long kiss, and it sent shivers down my spine and made my knees weak. So weak that I was grateful his arms were holding me up. When he pulled back and looked into my eyes again, I found myself leaning into him and kissing him again. I threw my arms around his neck and pulled him to me. I felt his tongue along my lips, trying to sneak past them to taste mine, but being blocked. I opened my lips slightly to let him in. When our tongues collided, it was electric. They danced together until I couldn't breathe anymore. I had never felt anything like it. I pulled away and gasped.

"Casey," he said softly as his arms surrounded me, held together in his hands behind my back, "I've been waiting a long time to taste you like that. You're so different from any girl I've ever known. You are beautiful, funny, and smart, and you aren't afraid to get dirty. I love that about you. I'm going to miss you when I leave. I need to spend every minute I can with you before I go. I hope you won't mind that."

"I don't mind. I'm going to miss you, too." He kissed me again, soft and sweet. "I wish there was a way you could come back before the summer's over."

"I don't know. I can try, but I spend August with my dad at his place. He's in Florida. I don't know."

"Well, let's just see what happens." He moved his hands up to my neck, and kissed me again. This time we were all tongues and moans. Kissing him made me lightheaded, and I found it hard to steady myself on my legs. I moved my hands up to cup his face. I was like a starved animal, and wanted to crawl inside him. His hands stroked my back, pulling himself into me. I was putty in his hands. I held him tight against me. His hands roamed over my back and to my hips and back up again. I grabbed his face, his hair. I couldn't breathe. It was as if he was my oxygen and I gasped to get as much of that lifeline as I could. I felt my temperature rise. Goosebumps formed on my arms. His touch burned my skin. I'm not even sure how much time we spent there kissing. Time just seemed to stand still. But then all of a sudden, he pulled away.

His breathing was heavy and labored, his eyes closed. "We better stop. I have to get you home." He grabbed my hand and pulled me up the beach towards the dune opening. I was in shock. It was as if a switch was turned off and it was just — over. He dragged me away. He didn't say anything else, just continued to pull me behind as he stormed up the beach, sticking his feet into his flip flops and then mounting his bicycle. Dumbfounded, I followed, wondering what I had done to cause this sudden change in him. My beautiful Prince Charming, who just swept me off my feet, in front of a beautiful moon, in what was paradise, had turned into a cold monster. "Let's go, it's late," he said as he started to pedal away.

I was stunned. And hurt. Was I that bad a kisser? I haven't had any practice, but it didn't seem like it was that difficult to do. What had I done wrong? I slipped into my flips, mounted my bike, and sliding onto the seat, turned it around. I shivered. I was embarrassed. He wouldn't look at me. I rode home behind him. He never looked back. We rode in silence. When we got to my street he looked back and said, "See you tomorrow," and rode off to Nick's. And that was it.

I pulled into my driveway, my eyes glistening with tears. I screwed up with Zack. I must be the worst kisser ever, and he decided that he needed to get away from me. I ruined my chances with him. He hated me. Stowing my bike in the backyard, I snuck quietly into to the back door, greeted only by a night light and Sasha. It was after midnight, and my parents were already asleep. I went to my bedroom, Sasha at my heel, and closed the door behind us. I threw off my sweatshirt and shorts and crawled under the covers in my underwear. I pulled the duvet over me and rolled into a ball. Sasha settled in next to me. I put my face into my pillow and cried.

"Nick, Nick, you up?" Zack snuck into Nick's room and tapped him repeatedly on the shoulder. Nick responded with a moan and looked up at him sleepily, trying to figure out where he was and who was poking him.

"Yeah, what's up?" Nick pulled himself from his stomach to a sitting position, rubbing his eyes trying to wipe the sleep from them and focus on the human form that was standing before him. "What's going on? What time is it?"

"It's me, and it's about one. I screwed up. I really screwed up." Zack sat on the bed next to Nick, his elbows propped on his knees, his head down and his hands rubbing through his hair. "I can't believe I did that!"

"Whoa, hold on Zack, did what? What did you do?"

"I screwed things up with Casey. I went too far. Then instead of apologizing, I just took off on her without any explanation. I mean, I had to leave, you know?" He looked at Nick, obviously upset with himself, and continued, "I started to get out of control. I would have done something that we both weren't ready for — especially not her."

"Zack, hold on. What exactly happened?"

"I took a walk on the beach with her. It was quiet. We were talking about how lucky we were to find each other. I told her I was leaving soon."

"Oh no, you didn't force her to do anyth . . ." Zack immediately cut him off.

"NO! No, nothing like that. But — but it almost got out of control. We kissed, you know? It was — nice. I could tell she hasn't had much experience kissing, but it was really nice. She's sweet. I kissed her again. She put her arms around my neck and pulled me close. I knew that if I wanted to, I could have had her right there on the sand. But I wouldn't do that to her, you know Nick?" He continued to ramble, as if he was trying to convince himself. "She's not like the other girls at home. She's — innocent. I really like her. I had to put a stop to it."

"So what did you do?" Nick put his arm on Zack's shoulder to try to calm him down a bit. "Is she okay? Where is she?"

"I rode home with her. Well, sort of. I just told her we had to stop and then left the beach. I couldn't explain it to her. I didn't have the words and I was mad at myself for feeling the way I did. I wanted to force her to the sand and touch her all over. I had to get myself out of there before that happened. I don't know what came over me! I know she hates me now!"

"She doesn't hate you. I'm sure she's wondering what the heck just happened, but she doesn't hate you. Casey isn't like that."

Zack turned to face Nick. Nick could see he was distraught, and his eyes were glassy and wet. "I would never have forgiven myself if something happened that she wasn't ready for, you know Nick? If she was one of the girls from school, then I wouldn't care. But she isn't like that. She's different. I'd never want to hurt her like that."

"I know, Zack. I know what you mean. That's how I feel with Phoebe. I think it's called respect. We respect them too much. But you have to talk to her. You can't let her wonder why you left her like that. She's probably upset."

"What could I say? That I didn't want to throw her on the sand and touch her all over her body? It's not the truth! I wanted to — I just couldn't!"

"Then you tell her that. Be honest with her. She'll respect you for making sure it didn't happen. But you can't let her think it was something she'd done to make you leave her like that."

"Crap! Crap! I screwed up big time!" He dropped his head back into his hands and dragged them through his hair, trying to calm his breathing. "Should I text her? I need to text her. What should I say?" He looked at Nick searching for an answer, but Nick had none to give.

"Yes, text her, but you'll have to figure out what to say. I can't help you with that." Nick threw himself back onto his pillow and pulled his legs up and under the covers. "I need to get back to sleep. I have lessons to give in the morning. Go back to your room. You'll think of something." He pulled the cotton quilt up to his shoulders and settled back to sleep.

Zack sighed and pulled himself off the bed and shuffled back to his room. He sat on the edge of his bed and turned on the small bedside lamp. Pulling his phone from his pocket, he fell backwards onto the pillow. Looking to the ceiling in hopes of finding courage and the right words to say, he laid there, arms outstretched and centering his breathing. Then he bolted up righted and began to type.

Text between Zack and Casey:

Zack: Hi. It's me. Are you okay? I'm sorry. I'm really sorry for doing that. Not for kissing you. But for leaving like that. I'm an ass. I'm so sorry. I didn't want to leave. I had to. Again, I'm sorry.

Zack hit the send button, and heard the sound indicating that the text was sent. He, waiting for a sign — any sign — that Casey read it. He hoped for a response, a text back that indicated that she was okay. He waited and waited. But nothing came. He fell back onto the bed holding the phone to his chest, waiting and waiting until exhaustion took him. And then he slept.

I turned my head when I heard the sound — the familiar ping that told me I had a text. Was it him? Was it Phoebe? Surely both Nick and Phoebe heard by now that Zack dumped me because I'm an inexperienced, horrible kisser and Zack can't stand me. They must think I'm a loser. I don't even want to see who it is. *What if it's him?* I don't want to know. I can't face him. Tomorrow's the party. I don't even want to go. I knew this would happen. Why did I even bother to get involved with anyone? I'm not ready for this summer romance stuff. It stinks. I hate it. And I hate Zack.

The next morning, I was greeted with a streak of sunshine peeking through my window, and a furry dog who wanted to go kayaking. It was early, and I hadn't really slept. So it looked like kayaking was what I needed to get my mind off of what happened last night, and give me some "alone time" to wallow in my loss. "Let's get out of here, Sasha," I whispered to her as I stroked her head which was resting on my leg. "Let's take the kayak out and get in some girl time."

I dragged myself out of bed, stripped out of the rest of last night's clothes and threw on a two-piece bathing suit. Glancing at my reflection in the mirror, I noticed a sadness in my face. From loss? I wasn't sure. But my legs felt like they were filled with lead and weighed a hundred pounds each. "Who needs him, Sasha, right? We got each other, girlfriend!" Sasha wagged her tail in anticipation and let out a quick bark to hurry me along. There was nothing she loved more than going out for a kayak ride, and I was taking too long for her liking. She wanted me to know that. "All right, I'm coming! Let's go get that kayak ready!"

Bounding into the kitchen, Sasha just about knocked my mom over as she carried the coffee pot over to the kitchen table to refill her cup. "Going out so early, Casey? It's not even eight o'clock. What time did you get in last night? I didn't hear you when you got back."

"I guess around one. We played mini golf after work. You'd never believe it — I won a free game by getting a hole-in-one!" Hopefully that would distract her from my foul mood.

"You're right," my mom smirked, "I don't believe it. You stink at that game." I let myself laugh with her, but it wasn't from my heart. I had absolutely nothing to laugh at today. Luckily, she didn't notice.

"I'm taking Sasha for a kayak ride. Be back later." I grabbed a black plum from the fruit bowl on the table as I walked by and shoved it into my mouth as we fled out the back door.

"Wear a life jacket!" My mom yelled to me as the screen door slammed shut behind me.

Our backyard was small, but it was packed with all the essentials needed when living at the Jersey Shore. You have your clothesline which strings across the yard for hanging wet bathing suits and towels, a small shed to hold your beach chairs, umbrella and various floating devices like plastic tubes and foam noodles, along with spare bike tires and air pumps, fishing poles, tackle boxes, skim boards, boogie boards, pails, shovels, nets for catching crabs, and traps. Usually there's a beat up surfboard stuffed into the rafters. Old bikes needing work usually found a home there as well. We had about three that we are always climbing over when we needed to find things. No yard would be complete without a picnic table with a big umbrella stuck through the middle where you sit to eat whatever you barbecued on the outside grill that night. Most yards also had some beach grass plants, but rarely did a beach house have grassy lawns. Here in Cranberry Cove you have rocks. Yellow or white rocks that make up your yard so there is never any mowing to do. You want to spend time at the beach, not behind a lawn mower. In my yard, there's also a blue ocean kayak.

The ocean kayak was a must at the shore. It's very floaty, and it isn't like the kayaks you see on freshwater lakes. Mine is a two-seater kayak, and has a little bit of space between the seats where Sasha can sit. Even though she weighs almost sixty pounds, she can still fit on this kayak along with two people. I love that I can use it by myself, too. It's easy to maneuver and as long as Sasha doesn't hang over the edge too much, it's easy to balance and keep from tipping over. With Sasha, I use the kayak in the bay because the water isn't too rough. But it's really fun to take the kayak into the ocean and ride the waves in it. It's challenging, and getting dumped out of it is half the fun. Not to worry today, though, since today we'd be heading to the bay, and the water will be very flat for a few hours until the boat traffic picks up and causes some chop. We should be back well before that happens.

I positioned the kayak onto the rolling wheels that would help me to get it down to the launch area. To get to the kayak launch ramp, we have to go to the end of the block and into the bay beach parking lot two blocks over. I grabbed Sasha's leash off the porch, and took a quick peek into the shed to grab my life jacket and one kayak oar. The oar has paddles on both sides of it. I tucked it on top of the kayak under a bungee cord. After attaching Sasha's leash to her collar, we were on our way out the back fence heading down the driveway to the street. Mom called out the front door, "Casey, you left your phone here, do you want it?"

"No, Mom, I'll get it when I get back. Thanks." I was briefly reminded that I received a text last night but never checked it. Whatever. I didn't feel in the mood to be in touch with anyone right now.

Sasha and I headed down the street, passing some neighbors and waving as they greeted us. The locals here have seen Sasha on the kayak and get a kick out of it. Usually I'm with Phoebe or Nick when I take her. Today it was just me and her. I waved and we continued on. The day looked to be shaping up to be a hot one, and it already had that stickiness in the air. Most likely there would be a few thunderstorms rolling through later.

The bayfront was really nice in Cranberry Cove. There were two docks that extended out into the water from the bay front parking lot. That's where the people who were vacationing would throw in a few crab lines and crab pots to try to catch enough blue claw crabs to make a pasta gravy, or to cook for dinner. There were rules for catching crab in New Jersey. The crabs have to be at least four and a half inches long from the points on each end of their shell. If they are a female crab, they have to be thrown back. The male crab has really nice blue coloring on their claws. Females usually have red on the tips of their claws. You can also tell the sex of the crab by looking at its underside. The female has a triangular shape etched into its shell, and the males have a shape that resembles the Washington Monument. At least that's what I called it when I first noticed it as a little girl.

To the right of the bayfront there were a few tennis courts and basketball courts that were always in use during the summer. Benches and water fountains placed nearby gave you a chance to refresh and catch your breath, watch the sailboats and windsurfers, and gaze at a garden of native plants and flowers that were maintained by the town's master gardener. It was very scenic, and provided a great front row seat to the spectacular sunsets that appeared in vivid color each evening as well.

Sasha and I rolled the kayak up to the launch ramp and prepared for our ride. I lifted the kayak off the wheels and placed them, along with my flip flops and Sasha's leash, to the side of the wooden fence by the water. Hopping in, I settled myself in the seat, and then signaled Sasha to join me. She was already excited, wagging her tail and barking as she hopped into her position. I used the oar to push us away from the launch, and we were off. The rhythmic rowing that would pace us would be a good distraction for me as I tried to clear my head and figure out what happened last night, and what I needed to do about it. As we made our way out into the bay, and passed the crabbing docks, children pointed at us and adults grabbed their cameras. There aren't many dogs here that enjoy kayaking as much as Sasha, and it is a sight to see. I took a moment to slow down my strokes to allow them to get a good picture, and lifted my hand in a little wave. They waved back. After a minute or two, I got back into my rhythm and we were heading out into the channel of the bay, away from the shore, away from Zack and what happened last night, and away from the humiliation of it all. The problem now was, would I have the strength and courage to paddle back in?

The breeze on my face felt good; refreshing, as if cleansing me and my thoughts from last night. I needed to revisit what happened in my mind without the emotion and feelings of doubt, to see what it was that went so wrong. The more I paddled, the more I felt my head clear, and after twenty minutes I seemed to come out of my daze and noticed that I'd paddled about a half mile offshore. To my left was a small island called Little Sedge, and it's where Sasha liked to roam and romp in the shallow water. I decided to take us in that direction. It would be empty at this time of morning except for the families of seagulls that nested there, along with swans, and schools of minnows and killies. It would be the perfect place to hash out what was on my mind.

As I neared the island's shoreline, I gave the okay for Sasha to exit the kayak. She waited for my verbal signal, then launched and jumped through the water. I pulled the throw toy out from under the seat and threw it for her to swim and fetch. With a deep sigh, I prepared myself to go back to last night and the events leading up to Zack's sudden departure.

I remembered how he told me he was going to miss me. I would miss him too. He seemed happy to hear me say that. He said I was lucky to live here. And he said he was lucky to know me. I remembered he pulled me to him, put his arms around me and kissed me. It was the kiss of someone who cared and not someone who wanted to take advantage of me or force himself on me. I wanted it as much as he wanted to give it — I knew that. I felt it in the way it was soft and loving. But then I did something. I threw my arms around his neck and made him kiss me again. Did he not like that? I remembered he kissed me back. But then he pulled away and said he had to go. What were his words? *We better stop.* I remember how he said it. *We better stop.* Like this is horrible and you don't know how to kiss so we may as well stop it now. *I have to get you home.* There are better things I wanted to do than stay here with you. *Let's go, it's late.* I can't waste my time with you here anymore.

The tears began to fall down my face. I crouched down and sat in the sand, my face buried in my hands. Why did I kiss him back? I must have looked like such a jerk throwing myself at him. He couldn't wait to get away from me. It was my fault. I pushed him away without even realizing it. I scared him away by kissing him back that second time. He hated me. And now I hated him. I hated him for how he left me there. I hated him for showing up in my life. And I hated him for saying that he would miss me. I won't miss him. I don't even want to remember him. And if he doesn't want to kiss me, I'll find someone who would. I'll find someone who won't leave me on the beach. And I'll do it tonight at the party. That was my plan. I was going to show Zack that I can kiss and someone will want to kiss me back. I just hoped he'd be watching when it happened.

"Ahoy, Casey and Sasha!" I heard a familiar voice as we made our way back across the bay in the kayak. It was Nick in a small sailboat giving a lesson to two young boys. He waved as he glided past, the two boys giggling at the sight of Sasha on the kayak.

"Hey, Nick! Nice day for a sail!"

"Got two more lessons after this. Don't forget the party tonight after work!" He was yelling but the sound was fading as the tiny sailboat took him and his passengers downwind from us, and out into the open bay.

"Okay, Sasha, time to get home and rest up. I've got a party to go to tonight." Sasha wagged her tail, nose into the wind, and I continued my rhythmic paddling as we cruised closer and closer to the shore.

Phoebe got back later than expected from visiting her grandmother, so I left for work without her, which was okay by me because I didn't want to discuss the fiasco with Zack from the night before. When I got back from kayaking, I read the text he left me last night and didn't understand it. He said he didn't want to leave, well then why did he? The fact was, he left me there. I didn't accept his apology. I didn't know if Phoebe knew anything about what had happened, and frankly, I didn't want to know. As far as I was concerned, it never happened. Today was a new day, and the new Casey would be making a debut — particularly at tonight's party.

The jingling of the bells above the door could hardly be heard over the crowd that was packed into the Polar Palace on this Saturday night. The Crabby Tuna was having a band and a magician for the kids, and the tourists were all over it tonight. The line never ceased, and when Phoebe did show up just ten minutes late, we were so busy we had no time to talk. I just nodded my hello, and she jumped into the spot at the register relieving the poor newbie girl who was barely hanging on. The newbie wasn't used to such crowds during the day shift, but she held up pretty well. I gave her the thumbs up and yelled a thank you to her as she retreated to the back of the shop to probably vomit before heading home.

The music wafting in from the Tuna tonight was a mixture of Springsteen, seventy's music, and country. This band somehow played it all, and the people were eating it up. It was one of those nights where you somehow knew all the songs, and each one sounded better than the last. The combination of the singing and the crowds made our shift fly by, and before you knew it, Nick appeared in the doorway.

"Time to go already?" Phoebe asked to no one in particular. "I can't believe we just worked four hours! Time to par-tay!" As I scooped my last cone, I noticed out of the corner of my eye that Zack was nowhere in sight, but I didn't want to ask. I figured he didn't want anything to do with me. Nick must have noticed my glance at the bike rack, and so he volunteered the explanation.

"Zack said he'll meet us. He's still not showered. He knows where it is. The three of us will go together, okay Casey?" By the look on Nick's face, he knew what was up. I didn't want him to know I was upset by it, so I tried to be as enthusiastic as I possibly could.

"Cool, yeah, Nick, sounds okay to me."

"Awww, I hope he doesn't take too long." Phoebe whined for no reason that I could see. It didn't seem to me that she knew anything, and I was happy to keep it that way. But she was a smart girl, and eventually I knew she'd figure it out. "Are we just about ready? Are you sure this kid isn't going to get into trouble for having friends over?"

"He said his parents are away and it's cool with them." Nick directed his response to both of us even though Phoebe asked the question. "So, let's go check it out. I know he has a ping-pong table, and said that he had people over all the time." Nick seemed to know this kid from school, so what was the worst that could happen? If it wasn't fun, then we'd just leave.

"I need to just refill some of the supplies. Why don't you two go ahead and I'll meet you. Give me the keys, Phoebes, and I'll lock up."

"You sure, Case? We don't mind waiting."

"I'm sure. You guys go on ahead. I'll be there in about ten minutes."

"Okay, you have the address, right? Thirty-five Oceanside. The house faces the beach. Don't take too long!"

"I won't. Save me a seat. I'll be there soon."

I watched as Phoebe and Nick hopped onto their bikes; Phoebe on the sherbet-colored bike, and Nick on a rusty old metal one. I think they looked cute together, like this could really work out for them. Nick was so sweet, and Phoebe was — well, she's Phoebe and I love her. But they aren't my problem right now. It's Zack. I wondered if the reason he wasn't here was because he didn't shower yet, or if that was just an excuse. I laughed to myself. *Yeah, just like my excuse that I needed to restock.*

I pulled up to thirty-five Oceanside, and I saw people all over the place. There were crowds of teenagers in the side yard, the front yard, spilling onto the boardwalk, and others crammed in the back yard. This side of town was far from the bustle of the stores, so there wasn't as much a bike police presence here. I thought to myself what Pauley would do if he rode up on this crazy scene.

I found a place to put my bike and walked around to the back of the house to see if there was anyone I recognized. Almost immediately, I felt an arm around my shoulder and when I turned, a smiling face next to mine. "Hey, you look like you just got here, and you seem to be missing something!"

"I am?" I asked him, shocked at how he could have even known I wasn't here earlier because of the sheer amount of people in the yard.

"You need a glass of my special punch! Here." He reached behind himself to the picnic table where a huge orange Gatorade cooler sat and he poured a glass of punch from the spout into a red party cup. He handed it to me with a flourish. "For you, Madame!"

"Thanks. And you are . . .?" I asked to try to get his name. Was this Nick's friend?

"I'm your worst nightmare, my dear!" And he laughed, pleased with his joke, and walked away. That was weird. But, I was thirsty from that shift, and we were so busy that I never had a chance to take a break to grab anything to drink. I gulped it down. It was delicious and cold, and tasted like Cherry Kool-Aid. I grabbed a refill before I continued on to find Nick and Phoebe.

The music was blasting as I peeked my head inside to look for them. The kitchen of this house was very pretty, and it was obvious that whoever owned it had money. Beyond the kitchen I saw a living room area with some couches, but I couldn't see who was in there, so I stepped inside in an attempt to make my way over. A very attractive guy who looked about Jase's age grabbed me by the wrist and stopped me in my tracks. "Do I know you?" he asked with a tilt of his head; his curly brown hair looking like he just got out of the shower. His eyes were a stunning blue, and seemed to pierce mine as he locked onto them.

"Ummm — I don't think so. I'm Casey, I live down the other end of town. And you are...?"

"I'm Mike. I'm a lifeguard here in the summer. I'm sure I've seen you around."

"You must know Jase. He's my friend's brother. Maybe you've seen me talking to him?"

"Yes, I know who you are! You're that girl who body surfs! Boob girl!" As soon as it left his lips, I could see his eyes widen as he realized what he'd just said. I froze. "Hey, look, I'm sorry. It's just that you're a good body surfer, but we didn't know your name. We had to call you something. I'm sorry. Really." He looked so apologetic, and I noticed he still hadn't let go of my wrist. I decided to let it slide.

"Yeah, it's Casey. So let's lose the other name, okay?" I gave him a smile in hopes that he'd see that I was a good sport about it. I glanced down at my wrist to let him know that he still had it locked in his grip.

"Oh, sorry! Yes, Casey, I promise to lose the other name. Forgive me?" And I looked at his eyes and melted. Yes, he was hot. His eyes had me spellbound. I nodded. "Can I get you anything? A beer?"

"A beer? No way! I don't drink beer!" I couldn't believe he'd even asked me that. Surely he knew I wasn't twenty-one, and he wasn't either. But I glanced into his party cup and he was drinking that same Cherry Kool-Aid that I was.

"Oh, you're drinking Matty's famous punch. Good for you. Can I get you some more?" He took my glass and topped it off.

"Thanks, Mike, I'm going to walk inside to see if my friends are in here, okay? I'll see you in a bit." I shuffled past him, and could feel his eyes on me as I walked away. I wondered if Jase was here. Maybe all the lifeguards were here. I stumbled past the rows of kids, and stumbled into the living room and where I spotted someone I'd seen before — Miss Blondie from the beach, and she was plopped in the lap of none other than the man himself. Jase was here. He spotted me.

"Beach Girl! You made it!" He raised his party cup to me. "Phoebe said you'd be coming!" He pushed Blondie off his lap and struggled to his feet and came over to me with a big hug. "Welcome to the party!" His arm was wrapped around my waist, and his party cup was held high as he swept it around as if it was a torch. He'd never hugged me before. What had gotten into him?

"Is Phoebe here?" I asked him, but yelled it over the music which was now thumping in my head.

"Yeah, she's here somewhere with Nick. I think they went outside or up to the beach for a walk. Come sit down by me. Have you met my friend Sarah?" So now I knew Blondie's real name, but I really didn't want to meet her. And I still didn't know why Jase still had his arm around me, leading me over to the couch. I tried to make a break. As much as I was enjoying the attention, I really didn't want to meet Blondie Sarah. And I noticed up close she was wearing way too much makeup. And her eyes were too close together. I didn't like her nail polish. I could have stood there and picked her apart all night. "Where's that guy you've been hanging out with, I think Zack is his name? You didn't bring him?" He was yelling in my ear and balancing his party cup up in the air, not worrying about spilling anything on the carpet.

"I think he's coming later. And I'm not with him or anything." I wanted to make sure Jase didn't think I was dating Zack, because I was not. I looked again at Blondie and noticed she was eyeing me up and down, her arms crossed across her chest, her right leg crossed over the other at the knee as she bobbed it up and down to the music, a scowl on her face. She obviously wasn't happy that Jase's attention had gone from her to me. I was feeling good about that. I just didn't like her with him. *Because I want to be with him?* I smiled to myself. *Yes, being with Jase would be really cool.*

I snapped back to the here and now, and I began to feel a little dizzy. Must have been the heat. And the crowd. It was definitely hot in the house from all the people, it was very loud, and I felt as if I needed some fresh air. I grabbed Jase's hand from my shoulder and whispered in his ear that I was going to go outside for a bit. It felt good to touch him. I'd never been this close to him before, other than the time he gave me mouth-to-mouth. He smelled good, and looked great. I looked over at Blondie and smiled before I headed back outside. "Don't be a stranger, Beach Girl!"

Jase yelled to me before he danced back to the couch and sat down next to a now grumpy Blondie Sarah.

The fresh air hitting my face felt good. I downed the last of my Kool-Aid and noticed Mike heading towards the steps, and me. "Hey, Casey, did you find your friends?" As he was asking, he was also grabbing my party cup and filling it with another round of Kool-Aid.

"Not yet, I heard they may be out here. Whoa." I felt myself teeter and lean a bit to the left, and then felt an arm as Mike grabbed me by the waist and led me over to a bench on the patio.

"Better sit for a minute. Looks like you drank too much punch. Matty makes it strong."

"Strong? What do you mean? Strong Kool-Aid?" I asked, not sure what he was talking about while watching the patio move beneath me. "I'm not feeling so well."

"Come on, I'll get you inside so you can lie down for a minute. You'll feel better after that." He helped me up and we pushed our way back into the house, bypassing the living room where the couches were and towards one of the guest rooms down the hall. As we passed the living room, I glanced in and caught Jase's eye as he was talking to someone. He stopped mid-sentence, jumped up from the couch and followed us. In what seemed like a flash, he was standing right beside me.

"Mike, what the hell are you doing with her?" I heard Jase say. He was following behind us as Mike led us down the hallway. At this point, I could barely grasp where we were, but I knew I needed to sit down. Mike's arm around my waist was the only thing holding me up right now.

"Cool it, Jase, I'm taking her to Matt's room. What do you care anyway?"

"You aren't taking her anywhere. Let her go!" He tugged at Mike's arm. I heard the agitation in Jase's voice, but couldn't quite understand what the fuss was about. I just wanted to lie down.

"If I let her go, she'll fall down. She's drunk out of her skull!" What? Drunk? How could I be drunk? All I drank was Kool-Aid! This couldn't be what I was hearing. Surely I was just dizzy from being hot. I hadn't really eaten much today.

"Leave her be. I'll take her." He reached for me, still trying to pry Mike's arm from around my middle.

"Go back to Sarah, Jase. This has nothing to do with you. You have your own Boob Girl." What? That I heard. I thought he wasn't going to call me that anymore? Why weren't we moving closer to the room where I could sit? I was starting to feel nauseous, like I was going to throw up. I needed to get to a bathroom. What was wrong with me?

"Ummm . . . can I use the bathroom? I don't feel so well." I seemed to mumble it, but no one was listening. Jase and Mike were still arguing. I grabbed Jase's arm. "I need the bathroom NOW!" I saw Jase's face as it registered, finally, that I was going to be sick.

"Shoot, Casey, over here, quick!" He grabbed me from Mike and pushed me into the bathroom just in time for me to throw up into the toilet.

"Gross! She's all yours now, bro!" I heard Mike say as he walked away. Jase closed the door behind us and locked it. He carefully grabbed my hair away from my face and tried to fill a glass with water from the sink. I continued to heave into the bowl.

"What's the deal, Casey? Why were you drinking? I didn't know you drink!"

"I'm not drunk! Why is everyone saying that? All I did was drink that stupid Kool-Aid! I didn't have any beer!" I continued to heave, but my stomach was emptied of everything that was in it. Sweat was pouring from my forehead, and my skin felt clammy and damp. Jase gave me the glass of water to sip. I sat on the floor next to the bowl, and Jase helped me to hold the glass as I sipped the water. This was not how I envisioned being in his arms at all — hanging over a toilet throwing up and feeling like crap.

"That punch is spiked with alcohol! Didn't you know that? Who gave that to you?"

"What? I didn't know that! I thought it was Kool-Aid!"

"Damn, Casey, you could have put yourself in a very dangerous situation! Don't drink anything at parties unless you know what it is!"

"I'm sorry! It's not like it was labeled! I've never even been to a stupid party like this before!" I started to cry. Jase took the glass from my hand and grabbed a towel from the rack and wiped my face.

"Don't cry, I'm not yelling at you. I'm just concerned. I'm glad I saw Mike dragging you down the hallway. I don't know what I would have done if something bad happened to you. And wait 'til I get my hands on him." He said the last part under his breath as if I wasn't supposed to hear it.

"I'm sorry for being so much trouble," I whimpered, my eyes looking anywhere but at him as I tried to hide my embarrassment. "I'm sure Sarah isn't happy with me or you right now."

"Forget Sarah. You're my only concern. Let's get you up on your feet. Can you stand up?"

I grabbed onto him and the bowl. He leaned over me to flush it. I still felt dizzy, but a bit steadier on my feet; however I had a headache to die for. People were banging on the door wanting to use the bathroom. Jase yelled for them to stop. "We'll be right out!" They yelled something back, but stopped banging. I looked at myself in the mirror, propping myself up on the sink to make sure my legs would be able to hold me. I looked horrible. I began to cry again. Then I heard Phoebe's voice. "Jase? Casey? Are you in there? Let me in!" Jase opened the door and Phoebe squeezed in. I looked past her and saw Nick and Zack in the hallway, trying to see what was going on. They looked worried. I quickly focused my eyes downward — I didn't want them to see me this way.

"What the heck, Casey? What are you doing? Are you sick?"

"She drank the spiked punch and didn't realize it had alcohol in it. Mike gave it to her. Luckily I saw her before anything bad happened."

"Bad like what?" They continued to talk about me as if I wasn't even in the room. I felt like an errant child being scolded by her parents, and wanted to just crawl out the window and run away from all of this.

"Mike was taking her into Matty's room. She had no idea — she couldn't even stand up on her own! I happened to spot him leading her down the hallway. I stopped him, but then she got sick."

"Casey! Oh my God! This could've been really bad! Where is that idiot? I'm going to go kick his butt!" Phoebe was fuming. I didn't want her getting involved. I just wanted to get out of there. I turned to Jase, who I noticed still had his arm around my waist for support.

"Jase, thank you for looking out for me. You get back to the party. I'll be okay. I'll stick with Nick and Phoebe. You go back and be with your friends."

"I'm not leaving you, Casey. Not until I know you feel better."

"I'm fine. Really. You go out. I'm going to hang here for a minute with Phoebe." He looked at Phoebe and she nodded her reassurance to him.

"If you're sure, then okay. I'll go. But don't go near the punch, and don't go anywhere near Mike!"

"Oh, don't worry about that!" I assured him as he slowly dropped his arm from my waist and left Phoebe and me alone. As soon as he opened the door, I saw Nick and Zack in the hallway jump up from where they were leaning against the wall, and Jase motioned them to follow him. "Great. Now everyone's going to know what happened. I just want to get out of here, Phoebes. Just walk me outside to my bike and you stay with Nick. I'm okay, really." She looked at me like she might have considered doing it, but then thought twice.

"No. No way. I'm going with you. Let's get you out of this bathroom, and we'll go up to the beach until you feel a bit better."

"I don't want to face Zack. Please. You stay here and just let me go off alone."

"No way, Casey! I'm not leaving you. Don't be a doofus. You and I will head up to the beach and then you can tell me what happened. The fresh air will do you good." She opened the door slightly to take a peek to check if the coast was clear, and luckily Nick and Zack were nowhere to be found. We tiptoed down the hallway to the front entrance, pushed our way through a group of kids, and stepped out onto the porch. It looked as if the amount of people at this party had doubled since I'd arrived, but before we could take a step forward, someone standing in the yard yelled "FIGHT!" and then chaos ensued. Groups of kids scattered and ran to the backyard, dropping cups as they went. Phoebe and I looked at each other and then crept over to the side of the house to see what was going on. Mike was in a fight with Zack. My Zack. Jase was trying to pull Zack away, but Zack had Mike in a headlock and was throwing fist after fist down on Mike's face. The crowd was cheering him on, and watching as Mike tried to twist himself out of Zack's grip while grabbing at Zack's legs. Zack threw Mike to the ground, yelling profanities at him and grunting with each punch he threw.

"YOU ASS! HOW DARE YOU TOUCH MY GIRL! WHO DO YOU THINK YOU ARE? IF YOU HURT HER, SO HELP ME, I'LL BUST YOUR HEAD AND YOUR LEGS AND . . . " Zack continued to pummel Mike, while Jase tried to pull Zack away.

"COOL IT! ZACK, LAY OFF!" Jase yelled at him. Nick jumped in to try to get Mike off the ground and break it up as well. Finally, Jase grabbed Zack around the waist and twirled him around and away from Mike, who was now just a rolled-up ball of clothes and flesh on the ground. Mike touched his mouth and pulled his fingers away, inspecting them for blood, huffing while down on all fours. Nick had his hand on Mike's back to steady him and to make sure he didn't charge back at Zack. Jase was talking in Zack's ear, trying to get him to calm down and breathe, but Zack just kept trying to pull out of Jase's arms, huffing and breathing with an open mouth.

Zack looked as if he was shooting daggers at Mike, and from the looks of Zack, he didn't feel that this fight was over yet.

"YOU BETTER STAY AWAY FROM HER!" Zack continued to yell at Mike, trying to raise his arm to point at Mike, while Jase continued to push Zack backwards and away from the scene.

"He's fighting over you, Casey! He found out what happened. Jase must have told him and Nick when he left the bathroom. Zack is ticked off!" I just stared, numb at the entire scene. Mike continued to spit at the ground, spatters of blood all around his lip and nose continued to drip onto the ground. His shirt was ripped, and his knees looked torn up from the cement patio he was kneeling on. Zack's eyes were big and round and looked possessed, not at all like the warm, caring eyes I remembered looking into last night at the beach. Zack's hair was a mess. His knuckles were bloody and red. He continued to shake them, trying to shake off the pain. Nick caught Phoebe's eye and let out a loud puff of air, a release, as the adrenaline that had worked up in his body finally settled. Nick helped lift Mike off the ground and to his feet, and brought him over to one of the picnic table benches. A girl brought over some ice from a nearby cooler wrapped in a t-shirt. She held it to Mike's face and he flinched, still taking deep breaths as he tried to calm himself down. Jase walked Zack to the front of the house, still whispering in his ear as a distraction.

Phoebe and I stayed on the other side of the house trying to comprehend what we had just witnessed. I felt as if my insides were going to make another appearance — tasting the bile as it crept up in my throat. I put my back against the house and sunk down until I was sitting with my knees up against my chest. I wrapped my arms around my legs and held them in place, sinking my face between my knees trying to steady my breathing. Closing my eyes, I focused on each breath as I willed my stomach to calm down. I faced the reality that I was the cause of this. It was my fault that this whole fight happened, because I drank the red Kool-Aid and didn't realize it wasn't really Kool-Aid. I had gotten myself into a dangerous situation that could have resulted in me getting assaulted, or raped. I shivered at the thought. If Jase hadn't seen me, what might have happened? How stupid could I have been? We learned about this in our health classes at school. How did I not realize what I was drinking? And now Zack had a fight because of me. What could possibly happen next?

It didn't take long for that question to be answered. No sooner had the question popped into my head, did we see three Cranberry Cove bike cops roll into the driveway and park their bikes, and one of them was Pauley. Someone must have called the police when the fight started.

Two of the cops were herded into the backyard by a group of girls. Pauley noticed Jase with his arm around Zack and headed over to them as they sat on the front porch. Could this get any worse? Phoebe began stroking my hair as I sat, numb and curled up, and she watched as Nick talked to the cops about the fight. They took little flashlights off of their utility belts and shined the light on Mike's face, assessing his injuries. They inspected his knees and the cut on his lip. One of them looked around the yard, noticing the red party cups and coolers. No doubt about it that underage drinking had been going on and someone was going to have to answer for it.

At that point, many of the kids began to leave the property. They certainly didn't want to be rounded up while parents were called and summonses were issued. Before long most everyone had left. Phoebe grabbed my arms and pulled me up. "Let's go talk to Pauley. We need to tell him what happened."

"No way! I'm not telling him what happened here tonight! Are you CRAZY? My mother and father will kill me!"

"He won't tell on you, but he needs to know. He's our friend, and we need to tell someone so Zack and Jase don't get into trouble. Come on, Casey! NOW!" Phoebe grabbed my hand and dragged me to the front porch where Pauley was examining Zack's hand. He was using a napkin to try to get some of the dried blood off of it. Zack's breathing seemed to be more settled now, and he didn't look like a crazy person anymore, he just looked exhausted. Jase saw us approach.

"Casey, are you okay? Phoebe? You didn't get caught up in this, did you?"

"No, we're okay. We were on the side of the house." Phoebe used her chin to point to where we were standing while the fight was happening. "Zack, are you okay?" Zack ignored her, instead, looking at me as my gaze took him in, unable to form any words at all.

"Casey, I'm sorry about last night. I'm so sorry I wasn't here to watch out for you tonight." He reached out to me, but I froze. He dropped his head and then looked back at me. "Are you okay? Did you get my text?"

"I'm . . . I'm fine, Zack. I should be asking you."

"I'm fine. I'm really sorry. I only left last night because I wanted to protect you so that nothing happened. I wanted you to be safe. I'm probably not saying this right, but I wanted to protect you from me. Can you understand that?" His words poured out with such sincerity, and as if no one else was standing here — just us.

My heart broke. He was apologizing to me. Here he was, a bloody mess from a fight on my behalf. I dropped Phoebe's hand and walked over to him and sat down on the porch steps next to him so that he would know how grateful I was for what he did. I didn't like it, but I understood what he did for me. He wanted to protect me. And that's what he did last night. He wanted to make sure that nothing got out of control or put me in a position where I would feel uncomfortable. I felt like crying again. How much more complicated was this going to get?

"Someone needs to tell me what this fight was about. I'm going to have to write a report, and unless someone has a good explanation, I'm going to have to take you all in and call your parents. You know I don't want to do that," Pauley stressed in his Bike-Cop authoritative way.

Jase stepped up. "I'll tell you. This kid threw a party. He made spiked punch. Casey didn't know and drank it. She got dizzy and Mike over there," he pointed to the back yard, "decided to walk her into a bedroom to take advantage of her. But he didn't get that far because I noticed what he was doing. I confronted him, and then she got sick. She ended up puking in the bathroom. When I got out, Nick, Zack and I confronted him and told him what we thought of him and his inappropriate behavior. Mike made some lewd comments about her, and Zack here stuck up for his girl. End of story."

"Did he touch you, Casey? In any way, did he touch you inappropriately or do anything to you that you didn't want him to do?" Pauley looked very serious as he questioned me and I looked him straight in the eyes as I answered.

"No, it was just like Jase said. We never made it to the bedroom. I got sick and Jase got me out of Mike's hands and into the bathroom in time for me to throw up. He never got a chance to touch me." Zack let out a sigh of relief, as if he was holding his breath the whole time awaiting my confirmation of the night's events. I was ashamed of myself for getting in that situation, and I told Pauley so.

Pauley looked at all of us, assessing his next move. Finally, he said, "You all should get out of here. I'm going to go talk to the kid who ran the party and this Mike character." He looked at Jase. "Get them home safely. Get some ice on Zack's hand. Somehow I don't think the other guy fared as well. Looks like you've got some right hook on you, kid."

"You should see the other guy!" Jase said, laughing but then noticing that no one else was laughing with him. "Okay, let's get out of here." Zack got up, slowly, a bit shakily, and we walked over to get the bikes.

"What about Nick? We need to get Nick!" Phoebe was frantic, looking at Pauley.

"I'll send him out. Give me a minute." He walked to the back of the house, and a minute later Nick appeared.

"Zack, you okay? Wow! You pummeled him good! He's gonna have two shiners and some nasty black and blues!" He wrapped his arm around Phoebe pulling her close. I walked over to Zack and put my arm around his waist. He leaned against me.

"You sure you're okay, Case?" he whispered to me.

"Yeah, I'm sure. Thanks, Zack, for everything. I'm sorry I didn't text you back. I didn't understand everything last night and I was upset. Now I get it."

"Casey, you are so special to me, and I won't let anything happen to you. That's the only reason I left last night. I should have explained it, but at the time I didn't know what to say. I'm so sorry I hurt you."

"No, I'm sorry that you were so upset, and for putting myself in such a bad situation tonight. I had no idea that punch was spiked. I feel horrible right now that all this happened. I feel bad you got into a fight." Once again, the waterworks turned on and a tear fell down my cheek. Zack took his thumb and wiped it away.

"No more tears over this. Please. Only smiles for the rest of my stay here. Okay? I just want to end my vacation here on a really happy note. Think we can do that?"

"Yes. I promise we can do that. Beach tomorrow?"

"Yes. Beach tomorrow. But Casey?"

"Yes?"

"Wear your one-piece."

"I promise." I slid onto my bike while I'm sure I heard Phoebe chime in:

"Doofus."

Sunday's arrival brought much excitement in town as this was the day the Fourth of July Fireworks Show and Concert would be held at the gazebo. Every year, visitors from all over the island flocked to the Cranberry Cove bay beaches to claim a spot to spread out a blanket or some chairs and listen to a patriotic song concert and then be entertained by a top-rate fireworks display. The festivities were one of the biggest draws of the summer season, and the Cranberry Cove Governing Body went all out, as usual, to make sure it was always a memorable event. This year the Mayor of Cranberry Cove would give a speech about the meaning of freedom, and then small American flags would be distributed to everyone in attendance as a souvenir. Since they needed volunteers to hand out the flags, Nick, Phoebe, Zack and I signed up to help. We were going to be attending anyway. We wanted to help out my mom who is very good friends with the Mayor's wife. She always asked us to volunteer to help in the different activities during the year, and this was no exception. We were glad to do it.

We didn't have to be there until seven o'clock, so that left us plenty of time to relax and recover from last night's party. Zack texted me in the morning to set up some plans for the day.

Text between Zack and Casey:

Zack: Good Morning, Sunshine! How are you feeling today?
Casey: Good Morning to you! Slight headache, nothing too bad.
Zack: Good to hear. :)
Casey: How's your hand?
Zack: Ugly! I won't be able to hand model for a while. lol
Casey: haha Poor thing!
Zack: I have to go to the store with Nick this morning. Beach later on?
Casey: Sure. I'll head up and stake a claim to a good spot with Phoebe.
Zack: Okay. We should be up there by around one.
Casey: Great. See you then.
Zack: Bye, beautiful!
Casey: Bye!

Text between Casey and Phoebe:

Casey: Phoebes! You up?
Phoebe: Yup. Just woke up.
Casey: Beach with me?
Phoebe: Nick's going to the mall with Zack for something.
Casey: Zack said they will meet us later.
Phoebe: okay. I'll be ready in about 30. Want to eat first.
Casey: okay. I'll stop off and pick you up then
Phoebe: okay. How are you feeling?

Casey: Stupid.

Phoebe: Get over it. It's over. Don't dwell. Headache?

Casey: A little

Phoebe: Does your mom know?

Casey: Don't think so. I'm hoping to see Pauley so I can get the scoop.

Phoebe: okay. Fill me in later. Bye!

Casey: :)

On Sunday mornings, my parents would go to breakfast at a local grille called Pam's. They served breakfast and lunch and it was usually packed. The decor was really kitschy and cute, and visitors just loved it. It was like eating in your grandmother's house, with sayings hanging on the wall along with cuckoo clocks and old photographs of Cranberry Cove's early days as a fishing village. There was one picture of the first group of lifeguards that ever worked at Cranberry Cove beach. Their uniforms were one-piece suits and all the men had moustaches. They looked so much older than the lifeguards we have at the beach now. I wonder if back in the day the lifeguards looked attractive? I can't imagine, but to each his own, I guess. With my parents out of the house, I threw on my robe and took my orange juice and cereal out to the backyard to see if I could catch a glimpse of Pauley and find out what the outcome was from last night. Luckily, he was out there reading the daily newspaper. I walked over to the fence separating our back yards and got his attention. I also needed to thank him, and apologize to him for what he had to witness. I'm sure he expected more of me than the drunken display he had a glimpse of last night.

"Hey, Paulie."

"Hey, Casey, how are you feeling this morning?" He came over the fence and kept his voice low, which I appreciated, but I told him that my parents were out to breakfast. "You get home okay last night? That was quite a scene at that house."

"Yeah, I got home okay. Thanks for helping us out. I really had no idea what I got myself into. Did anyone get into any trouble?"

"Well, Mike was pretty beaten up. We had the first aid stop in to check out if he needed any stitches, but he didn't. He's got a lot of black and blues this morning I imagine! That Zack really took him to task!"

"Yeah, well, I wish he didn't do that. I don't want anyone getting into any trouble."

"I'm glad that Jase was sharp enough to see what was going down. You owe him a thank you for that. And Zack just wanted to avenge his lady. Nothing wrong with a guy sticking up for his girl. I just wish he had a bit more self control. Words probably would have done the trick instead of using his hands. But, no charges are going to be filed. We got Mike to drop charges against Zack in exchange for not charging him with giving a minor alcohol. We stayed and made everyone who was left at the party clean the place up. Took about an hour. I think they learned their lesson."

"I appreciate that, Pauley. I really do. I didn't tell my parents, and I hope they don't find out how stupid I was."

"I won't tell. Just be more careful. Nothing wrong with going to a party. Just be smart about it, okay? Won't be the last time you'll be at one of those, so use your noggin! Or else you'll have me to answer to!" In big brother fashion, he took his hand and palmed my head like I was five. I smiled and thanked him again, grateful that none of my friends would be in trouble for what took place last night. Pauley headed back to his newspaper and I shuffled myself back inside to finish my breakfast. *Whew! Crisis averted.*

The beach was packed, as I imagined it would be. A blue summer sky with no clouds in sight meeting a dark blue sea made for a perfect backdrop as families sat almost elbow to elbow along the sandy shoreline. Seagulls circled above the surf in search of a lunch treat of minnow or snapper, and cried out to each other as they lazily soared and then dipped towards the water. Children were busy digging holes in search of buried treasure or shells, and the small waves of low tide rolled lazily towards the beach leaving an array of colorful stones and bits of shells in its wake. The water temperature was in the low seventies, a treat for swimmers this time of year.

Phoebe and I parked ourselves just behind the lifeguard stand, and I was happy to see that Mike was not on duty at this post today. Jase and his usual partner, Jessica, were sitting high in the wooden seat, sunglasses and sunscreen on, gazing at the water. I walked over once I had my chair set up because I needed to thank Jase for what he had done for me last night.

"Jase, I just wanted to thank you again for last night. I don't know what I would have done if you didn't step in. Thank you again."

He peered down at me from his perch, his Ray Bans sitting low on his nose as he peeked over them. "Beach Girl, no thanks necessary. I'm just happy you're okay. How are you feeling?"

"Better. I woke up with a headache, but it's gone now."

"That's called a hangover. It won't be your last, I'm sure. But I'm happy you're okay." He winked at me, and then leaned over to whisper something to me. "I saw Mike this morning. He looked horrible! The boss told him to take a few days off. Zack really did a number on him."

I gasped, once more picturing the battle that I witnessed last night and the words that Zack was yelling as he continued to beat Mike to the ground. *How dare you touch my girl! You better stay away from her!* I shook my head to erase the images that popped up. "Well, I just wanted to tell you how much I appreciated you being there for me. I hope that I didn't ruin anything with Blon . . . I mean, Sarah."

"Ha ha! No, Beach Girl, no worries there. I told Sarah that we were friends, and she had to get over it. We're good. I'm just happy that you're okay. No more parties unless you tell me, okay? Someone's got to be there to keep an eye on you!" With that, I nodded and headed back to Phoebe who already was digging into the snack bags she packed and thumbing through her gossip magazine checking out what the celebrities were wearing about town last week.

"All good?" she asked as I plopped into my chair.

"Yeah, all good. I needed to say thanks. He really saved me."

"Ugh, don't get all 'knight in shining armor' on me now! You read too many of those stupid romance beach novels!" She licked her thumb and flicked the page over in a very exaggerated way and I laughed. "You never did tell me what happened with Zack. Nick said that you two had a falling out the night before. What happened when we left you alone after mini golf?"

It was time to spill the beans about what happened, and I was hoping that Phoebe would be able to help me make sense of it. "We walked up to the beach, and he told me how much he was going to miss me when his vacation was over. I told him I was going to miss him too. We kissed, and then we kissed again. It was good. I don't know what came over me, but I threw my arms around his neck and pulled him close and kissed him again, like I was out of control. At first, he kissed me back, but then he just pulled away and said that we had to leave. I thought it was because he didn't like the way I kissed. But last night when we sat on the stoop at Matt's house, he said that he was protecting me from *himself*. Now I understand that he wanted more and didn't want to force himself on me. I have to tell you, Phoebes, that if he did, I'm not sure I would have been able to say no."

"Wow, Casey, I'm stunned! You go from no boyfriend ever, to one who can't get enough of you! You hit the jackpot!" The envy in Phoebe's eyes as she stared at me was obvious. I guess Nick hadn't yet been that intimate with her, and she was a bit jealous.

"I don't see it that way, Phoebes. I'm grateful that Zack is a gentleman and had some self control. Anyway, he texted me when he got home that night, but I was so mad and upset that I didn't even look at my phone. I didn't look at the text until the next afternoon. The problem with that is I went to that party last night determined to get back at Zack for not wanting to kiss me. I'm afraid that even if I wasn't drunk, if Mike brought me into that bedroom alone, I may have done something I would be regretting today. I owe Jase big time for stepping in."

Phoebe pursed her lips and I thought now she understood what I was feeling about all of this. "Revenge in any form is dangerous," she said to me. "I see now why you've been so upset. Zack wanted nothing more than to protect you, and keep you safe. He would have killed Mike last night if Jase hadn't pulled him off. Wow." She reached out and touched my leg in a gesture that showed she understood how I felt. "Give him some slack. He's leaving in a few days and wants to spend time with you. You know he respects you — he's shown that twice now — once when he was with you, and then again when he thought Mike disrespected you. He's a keeper, Case. Enjoy him while he's here."

"I know, and I will. I hope he forgives me. I feel like I betrayed him by going to that party willing to make out with someone for spite. I feel horrible about that."

"He doesn't have to know about that. Just move on and make this right with him. Maybe before summer ends, he can come back. So don't throw it all away over a fear about something like this."

"You're right. I know you're right. I hope he forgives me for what happened." I slumped back into my chair and pulled my latest beach read out of my bag and got lost in a story about love, flowers, and first kisses.

"Who's up for a swim?" Nick plopped himself onto Phoebe's back and acted as if she wasn't even there.

"Ouch! Get off me!" she giggled and pushed at him as he proceeded to fight her off. Zack settled his chair in the sand right next to mine and sat down, smiling at me and offering a quiet hello. I noticed he had picked up quite a bronze tone to his skin over the past week, and it complemented the blond highlights that now streaked his curly hair. He grabbed onto my book and turned it in my hand to read the title.

"Hannah's Goodbye," he read aloud. "Sounds like a tear-jerker. Any good?" he asked as if he was genuinely interested, which I knew he wasn't. I giggled and hit him playfully with it. He acted as if he was injured. We both laughed.

"What say we all get wet? It's hot out here!" Nick finally removed himself from his seat on Phoebe's back and she pushed off the sand that he deposited on her and the blanket. Nick pulled off his shirt and threw it onto Phoebe's head in playful way, and then sprinted down to the water.

"You'll pay for that!" she yelled at him while she sprinted after him.

"You want to go in?" I asked Zack who remained seated next me, making no attempt to move or get up just yet.

"Can we talk first? I want to say something to you, if that's alright."

I twisted in my seat to face him and closed my book, placing it back in my bag to give him my full attention. This looked serious, and he obviously had something to get off his mind. I needed to say something too, but I wanted to let him go first. Once my eyes met his, he started. "First, I want to apologize again for how I acted Friday night. I never should have left you like that without explaining. I just didn't know what to say. My mind was saying stop, and my hands weren't listening. I needed to walk away before I did something that would have hurt you. Do you understand that?" He looked at me, reached for my hand that was resting on the arm of the chair. I looked down at his knuckles and saw the cuts and bruises, evidence of last night's brawl. I nodded a firm yes, but didn't speak. I didn't want to interrupt him now that he was on a roll. "Good. I needed to say that first. I care so much about you, Casey, and I wouldn't want anything to ruin my chances with you. Now, second, I want to apologize for not picking you up from work last night and taking you to that party. I was a coward. I didn't hear back from you when I texted you so I was afraid to face you. If I just had acted like a man, I would have apologized to you at work, and then we could have gone to the party together. I was afraid to see you and didn't know what to say. As a result, you ended up in a situation that could have been avoided. I take full responsibility."

"What? What I did last night was not your fault at all! I was the one stupid enough to drink the Kool-Aid. I was the one who went there looking for trouble because I was mad at you for leaving me on the beach. I thought . . . I thought . . ."

"You thought what, Casey?"

I looked down at his hand, then covered it with my other hand and squeezed, hoping the connection would give me the strength to tell him the truth about what I thought happened on the beach. "I thought you didn't like the way I kissed, and wanted to get away from me." It took all the strength I could muster to hold back the tears that were pushing against my eyes, looking for release. I felt my throat begin to tense and tremble. I swallowed and kept my eyes away from his and cast downward on his hand that I held in mine.

"How could you even think that?" he whispered as he turned further into me and pulled my hand up to his lips, holding it there. "I love the way you kiss. I've never kissed anyone and felt the way I do with you. Every time I look at you I want to kiss you. You are like candy to me, Casey. I don't ever want you to think that I don't like how you kiss. I was afraid that the kissing was going to lead to something else, and that's why I ended it. Please, don't ever think I don't want to kiss you." He leaned over and brushed his lips softly against mine, closing his eyes and then pulling back slowly as he once again gazed at me.

"Zack, I'm so sorry! I should have never gone to that party. I should have never let that Mike kid give me something to drink. I had no idea that the Kool-Aid was spiked. I'm so stupid!" The tears fell, and I wept, dropping my head to my knees. Zack released my hand and put his arm around my shoulders, comforting me, reassuring me that what happened was not my fault, and that he was so grateful that Jase was there for me.

After a long pause, he continued. "When Phoebe asked if anyone had seen you, a girl said you were in the bathroom with Jase. She knocked and when you let her in, I could see you were upset. It was torture waiting there in the hallway to find out what you were upset about. When Jase came out and told Nick and me what happened, I went to find that punk to give him a piece of my mind."

I lifted my head and sniffed, "And your fist."

He laughed. "Yes, and my fist — unfortunately for him." His smile left his face, and once again he looked me in the eye. "I would do anything to protect you, Casey. And if he would have hurt you in any way, he wouldn't be alive to talk about it today. Believe me."

My heart melted as he poured out his feelings about me. How was I so lucky to have let this guy into my life? I wanted nothing more but to let him know that I felt the same, so I leaned in and kissed him. I had no words to say to him that could have spoken for my heart any better than that kiss, and he knew it. He smiled and pulled my hand to his lips again and kissed it as he locked eyes with mine. We were done apologizing. Our conversation was now over, and we both understood the outcome.

"Let's go swimming." He pulled me to my feet, and hand in hand, we headed into the water.

Relaxing that afternoon in the company of my good friends, and Zack, of course, was such a treat. We enjoyed many laughs, some ice cream from the local vendor truck, and even a game of Frisbee. The sun continued to shine down on us all day, and by late afternoon the crowds at the beach began to thin. Phoebe and Nick were sprawled out on her blanket napping in the warmth of the breeze. Zack and I sat in our chairs, his fingers entwined with mine as our hands rested on the wooden arm between us. He was reading Phoebe's gossip magazine, and I was reading my novel. It seemed like a perfect ending to a perfect afternoon. Zack stroked my fingers softly as if to remind himself that I was indeed still sitting there with him. I put my head back and closed my eyes, relishing the feel of his hand on mine. Is this what love feels like? I surely didn't know the answer, but whatever this was, I liked it a lot.

"We better get going. It's almost five o'clock, and we need to be at the gazebo at seven," Phoebe said while she yawned and hatched from her nap. She sat up on her heels — legs folded beneath her and looked over at Zack and me. She noticed his hand on mine and gave me a "way to go" smile. Zack looked up from his magazine and sighed.

"Only one more day before I go back up north. I can't believe how fast these two weeks passed." Bending his elbow, he lifted my hand in his and spoke to me as if we were the only two people here. His fingers continued to play with mine, rubbing my knuckles softly. His gaze lingered on my face as I turned my head to take in his. We just stared at each other with silly grins on our faces, lost in the moment. Phoebe watched with her hands on her hips until she couldn't watch any longer.

"Okay you two lovebirds! Enough! I'm going to puke over your cuteness! Start packing up!" She got up in a huff, tapping Nick's leg with her foot until he finally began to stir. "Come on, Nick, time to pack up. Get your butt off the blanket. I need to get away from these two over here!" Nick glanced over at us and laughed. I pulled my hand out of Zack's and started to get up to pack. I put my book in my bag, and slipped my shorts on over my bathing suit. Zack got up and folded up the chairs and handed Phoebe back her magazine. It only took a few minutes to gather our things and we headed up the beach to the boardwalk. We each found our flip flops that were tossed at the entrance and shuffled over to our bikes. Agreeing to meet at the gazebo at seven o'clock, Phoebe and I rode off in one direction, Nick and Zack in another, all of us heading home to shower, change and eat dinner.

By six thirty, the parking lot at the bayfront was already filled as concert-goers began to lay stake on part of the lawn surrounding the gazebo. It looked as if the beautiful sunny day we enjoyed was just a prelude to the gorgeous sunset that would undoubtedly occur over the bay, just beyond the gazebo. Everyone who watched the concert tonight would be in for a treat as Mother Nature would direct the sun to say farewell to Cranberry Cove in a most spectacular way. Phoebe came to my house and together we walked down the street and over to where the Mayor's wife was opening the boxes of small flags that we would be distributing. She was happy to see that we'd arrived a bit early, and thanked us by instructing us to open the boxes and fill the baskets we would soon be carrying to distribute the flags to tonight's guests. With a few last minute instructions to us, she stepped away, leaving us to our task. In about fifteen minutes, we'd be walking around the bayfront handing out flags to everyone to wave during the concert and fireworks.

Nick and Zack arrived just as the last of the flags were loaded into the baskets. With such a large area to cover, it would be unlikely that we'd see each other during the concert. We each decided to take a different area so that we didn't miss anyone. The Bike Cops were already shutting down the street ends that flowed to the bay front road in order to keep the crowds safe as they walked with families and small children to their viewing spot. Pauley rode by and stopped to say hello on his way to his post. He asked Zack about his hand, and told Zack about the deal with Mike not to press charges. Zack seemed relieved, and thankful.

We decided to all meet up again over on the bay beach where the overturned Cranberry Cove rowboat was. It would be a great spot to view the fireworks and listen to the concert. I was secretly hoping that Zack and I would be able to catch the sunset from there, if our flags were all handed out. Since we'd left the beach this afternoon, I was already missing him, and wanted to feel his hand in mine again. I wanted to be next to him and to look at his eyes and his smile. I was finding it difficult to think about anything else other than Zack lately. He occupied my every thought. This was something new to me, and I was enjoying the feeling of butterflies in my stomach when he was around me.

We each grabbed a basket and headed out to begin handing out our flags. I loved walking through the crowds, seeing the families, friends and neighbors who had gathered together on this night every year. As the loudspeakers overhead began to screech, the crowd hushed as our Mayor took to the gazebo stage to welcome everyone and begin his speech.

"Welcome, everyone, to our annual Fourth of July Celebration! Mother Nature has gifted us a beautiful evening as we gather in celebration of our nation's independence, and to enjoy the wonderful sounds of patriotic music presented by Cranberry Cove's own symphony band. After we watch a glorious sunset over our beautiful bay, we'll all enjoy some fireworks!

Over two hundred years ago, our forefathers envisioned a great nation that would provide everyone the right to life, liberty and the pursuit of happiness. Cranberry Cove is my little piece of happiness here at the

Jersey Shore, and I suspect it's yours as well. Thank you for being a part of our town, and I hope all of you have a wonderful Fourth of July." With that, the band began to play a rousing "Yankee Doodle Dandy" and the crowd cheered and began singing along. It was a great warm-up to what would be a wonderful concert. The symphony knew how to put on a show.

I strolled through the crowd, handing out my flags to kids, parents and grandparents. They waved the flags to the music as the symphony played one great song after another. When they finally got to the part where they honor each leg of the armed services, I got goosebumps. The conductor asked that as each song was played, members of that group of the armed services should stand and be recognized. When they played the Marine Corps song, I saw my father stand and my mother crying. It was a proud moment for him to be recognized as a past member of the service. I looked at the men and women standing and I couldn't help but tear up. All ages of past and present members were cheered on by the audience. Each of them was proud to have served their country in whatever capacity they were asked. The conductor guided the symphony members through the songs of each service group: Navy, Army, and Air Force. It was probably the most moving part of the entire concert.

With all of my flags given out, I wandered over to the rowboat to wait for the others. It wasn't long before they arrived. We settled onto the sand, leaning back against the boat and watching the sun as it began to sink below the horizon. The sky was painted in pinks and purples. I watched as Nick put his arm around Phoebe, and then Zack positioned me to sit between his legs and lean back onto his chest. His arms were wrapped around me like a blanket, and his nose was in my hair, breathing me in. I wrapped my arms over his as they settled around my stomach. I felt warm and safe. The conductor instructed the audience to gaze out over the bay at the sunset while they played and sang "God Bless the USA." It was another one of those tear-jerker moments. Zack swayed back and forth slowly to the music and hummed in my ear. I was in paradise.

It was still about thirty minutes before the fireworks would begin. The music was great, and we all just enjoyed being there in the moment. Zack whispered in my ear that he had something to give me. "I want you to keep this and think of me when you wear it. I won't be around you, but this will remind you that I'm always thinking of you." He held out a little box wrapped with a pretty little bow. I looked back at him with surprise. "Go ahead, open it. I picked it up today. I wanted to give you something to help you remember the time we spent together." With shaking hands, I took the box from him. I pulled on the little ribbon and watched as it fell gracefully to the sand. I opened the lid. The beautiful charm bracelet inside took my breath away. I carefully lifted it out of the cotton bed in which it sat, and Zack took the box from me, allowing me to inspect it more closely. It had tiny dangling charms attached to its wide oval links. There was a wakeboard, a flip flop, a bicycle, and a golf ball. My finger stopped on the tiny silver ball, admiring its tiny little indentations. "In honor of your hole-in-one," Zack whispered as if he had read my mind. "The last charm is an 'X.'" I looked back at him, questioning. "Your kiss. To remind you how much I loved kissing you." I leaned into him to allow him to kiss me. "See? They are candy to me, Casey."

"Oh, Zack, I love it so much! Thank you for this bracelet. It's so beautiful, and the charms are perfect. Each one is special. Again, thank you!" He took it from my hands and carefully opened the clasp and wrapped it around my wrist. It dangled so perfectly and looked beautiful against my skin. It truly was one of the most thoughtful gifts anyone had ever given me. "When did you get this?" My smile was so wide it was hurting my cheeks.

"Today, when Nick and I went to the mall. I wanted to get something for you, and when I saw this, I knew this was the only gift to get. I think it perfectly sums up my two weeks here with you, don't you?"

"Absolutely!" I looked back at him, finding it difficult to tear my eyes away from the sight of my beautiful new bracelet. "I love it, Zack. Thank you again." I snuggled back into his chest and examined my bracelet as the daylight disappeared, and nighttime crept into the sky.

BOOM! The first crack of a firework being launched filled the air, followed by the bright starburst of yellow and red that lit up the blackness overhead. The audience cheered approval at the colors and spectacle as more and more flashes appeared over the bay. The fireworks show was spectacular and we watched without speaking, just soaking in the smells and sounds of an evening that I was sure I would remember forever. Zack held me close and whispered in my ear how much he loved sharing this time with me. I stroked the "X" charm on my bracelet, and pressed it between my thumb and finger, knowing what it represented, and it brought me back to that night on the beach when Zack had held me close and kissed me with such excitement. Zack's lips fell to my neck, and I could hear him breathing next to my ear. Soft lips touched me there, and then he pulled me closer into him as he rested his head on top of mine. We watched until the fireworks were no more, and we didn't move as the crowds picked up their blankets and chairs and headed for home. We just sat and enjoyed being together, hand in hand, in Cranberry Cove.

A rumble of thunder in the distance signaled that our night would soon come to an end. Reluctantly, we got up and brushed the sand from our shorts. Phoebe and Nick walked over toward the sidewalk, but when I tried to follow, Zack pulled me back. "One more kiss for the road, Casey, so I remember this night with you forever." I went willingly into his embrace and we kissed. I let his tongue past my lips and it began to dance with mine. His breathing began to change and I felt my own heart beating faster in my chest. His hands began to move up my back, and come to rest on my neck as he held my head in position. I grabbed at his waist and pulled him closer to me until our bodies touched. His breath hitched and he pulled away from the kiss and rested his forehead against mine. With his eyes closed, he whispered to me, "I can't be this close to you. I feel things that make me want to do more than kiss you. I can't let that happen. Not yet. I want you to understand that, Casey. We aren't ready for that yet. Do you understand?" He waited for me to answer. I did understand. I understood that I had no more will power left. I understood that what he made me feel when he kissed me is something I'd never felt before. I understood that we couldn't let this go any further. He was waiting for me to say something.

"I understand, Zack. You make me feel out of control. When you're near me, I can't think straight. I can't control myself. I understand we need to stop. I get it." I looked up into his eyes. They were glassy and beautiful and he was still holding my face in his hands. "I understand." I wanted him to know that I knew it took a lot for him to stop us and say that to me. He didn't want to have the same misunderstanding we had Friday night when he left me on the beach. I leaned in and gave him a quick kiss. "Come on. There's a storm coming and we have to get home."

28

Phoebe jumped into the twin guest bed I have in my room, while I sat on the floor with my back leaning up against it as Sasha sprawled out at my feet. Even though she lived only a few doors down from me, she would often sleep over so we could get some real good girl-talk time in. As we sipped our hot tea and the thunderstorm rumbled overhead, the conversation centered around Zack and Nick. "So did you almost faint when he gave you that bracelet? Let me see it again!" She pulled my hand toward her like it wasn't attached to my arm and through a squint she thoroughly examined each little charm attached to it. "Ugh, he's so romantic! I wish Nick were more like that." She plopped my arm back down into my lap and leaned back on the bed.

"How are things going between you two? I've been so busy with Zack and everything else that's happened. I haven't really had a chance to ask you."

"Oh, it's okay. Nick isn't much into public displays of affection. As a matter of fact, I usually have to grab his hand in public. I guess he's just shy or something. Nothing like you and Zack. Man, the way he looks at you. There is no mistaking how he feels about you. It's crazy, Case!"

"I know. When he looks at me with those brown eyes and that smile, I just … melt. I don't know how else to describe it."

"That's LOVE, babe! You are smack dab in the middle of your first crush! I never thought I'd see the day!" Phoebe snatched the pillow from under her head and put her arms around it and kissed it as if it were a person, making loud smacking noises. "Oh, Zack, I love the way you kiss!" She mimicked me, and I couldn't help but laugh at her silly acted-out make-out session.

"Please don't tell me that's how you kiss, Nick! That poor guy!" I laughed back at her. "No wonder he doesn't want to hold your hand in public!" We both giggled until we could hardly take a breath. "Seriously, though," I said as we finally calmed down a bit from our fit, "I'm really going to miss Zack when he leaves on Tuesday. Tomorrow's our last day together. I have a feeling I won't see him after that. Over the winter he'll forget all about me. I'm not sure how I feel about that."

"You don't know that he'll forget about you. And if you don't see him this year, then he'll come back and stay with Nick again next year. He's crazy about you, Casey. There is no way he'll forget about you!"

"He's fifteen going on sixteen. Are you telling me that there aren't a dozen girls up there in North Jersey wanting to get their hands on him? I can tell the way he kisses that he's had a lot of experience. I know he's had a girlfriend because he told me about her. I can't compete with that."

Phoebe smiled, but then the smile left her face and she got quiet. "I wasn't going to say anything, but Nick told me a little about him. He used to get into a lot of trouble. I think he was upset about his parents divorcing and he acted out a lot in school. His mom made him change schools, and that's how Nick met him. The old school was in a rough neighborhood with drugs and gangs and stuff. Zack wasn't in a gang, but he tried some drugs and even got arrested one night for breaking into some type of warehouse or something. But since Nick's known him, he hasn't been into anything like that. And that girlfriend was from his old school. She was trouble, Nick said. She cheated on him with some older guy. And now she's pregnant."

"How does Nick know that?"

"Zack told him about it. She was bad news."

"I don't like thinking about Zack being with someone like that. He's never made me feel ... pressured. In fact, it's the opposite. He's always the one putting the brakes on our make out sessions."

"You're really lucky, Casey. It's so obvious how much he cares about you. I mean, he almost pummeled Mike to death over you!" I took a minute to think about what Phoebe had just said. There was no doubt that Zack cared about me. I could see it in the way he spoke to me, and how he treated me, and how he was so careful that I didn't feel pressured into doing anything I wasn't ready for. My fingers stroked through Sasha's fur as I thought about our last kiss at the bay after the fireworks. *I am lucky.*

Monday morning came and went; the few showers that passed through on the tail end of the thunderstorms last night were just now making their way off the coast, and the sun began to peek out. By noon, the beaches began to fill up again, and life in Cranberry Cove went back to normal.

Today was my last day with Zack. Tomorrow, he would be heading back north to his mom's house, and then leaving for a trip to see his mom's family. After that, he'd be off to Florida to spend time with his dad, and then finally back home to start school. Summer would be over.

Phoebe and I were going to be working tonight, but this afternoon we decided that instead of going to the beach, we'd go out with Nick and Zack in the Splitz and do some crabbing. Poor Zack had never eaten a blue claw crab, so we were determined to have him enjoy the experience while he was here.

Nick had the Splitz all ready by the time Phoebe and I arrived. It was our job to bring the bait, so we stopped off at the market to pick up some fresh bunker and a package of chicken legs. Don't ask me why crabs like chicken, because it just doesn't seem natural, but they do. I guess it's because a chicken leg might resemble a seagull, and I'm sure plenty of dead seagulls end up in the bay and get eaten by crabs. I mean, the dead seagulls have to die somewhere, right? I don't know what makes me think about these things, but when I tried to discuss the topic with Phoebe, she winced. "Gross, Casey, enough about dead seagulls! You don't expect me to carry this smelly bag, do you?" She pushed the bag from the market in my direction as she twisted her nose and gave me a look.

"It's frozen, Phoebes, it doesn't smell . . . yet. Just wait until the sun bakes on it a little while! Yum!" I teased her and turned my hand in circles over my belly, the universal sign for good food.

"Ahoy! Let's get this show on the road!" Zack yelled as we pulled up and parked our bikes at Nick's boat slip. "I can't wait to see what we catch!" Zack's excitement was very evident as he helped each of us onto the boat just in time for Nick to begin backing out and before you knew it, we were on our way.

Cruising slowly through the lagoon in Nick's boat was so relaxing. The slow ride past the large homes allowed for some great sightseeing. Just about every house on the water had a boat tied up to a dock, and a pool, and beautiful landscaping. It was fun to imagine what it might be like to live in a house like that. My house is pretty average, and while it's big enough for my mom and my dad and me, I often wondered what it would be like to live in a huge house with lots of rooms filled with brothers and sisters. I sometimes thought about how lucky Phoebe was to have Jase, although all she does is complain about him. It must be cool to have someone else close by to keep an eye out for you.

Nick rounded the corner to the last lagoon and into view popped the Barrier Island Bridge. He yelled to us to hold on as the open bay allowed him to hit the gas and we began to cruise further away from the houses and closer to the bridge. The channel markers led the way so we didn't venture into the shallow areas and ground ourselves. It's happened before, and propellers can get expensive to replace, so captains learn quickly to stay within the markers in order to keep from hitting bottom. All four of us rode in silence, since the humming of the engine made it difficult to have a real conversation. We all seemed to be okay with that, and we just enjoyed the ride and the feel of the wet breeze as we made our way closer to the bridge.

As we neared one of the support pilings, Nick instructed me to grab the anchor and lower it to set. He cut the engine once he was sure that the anchor has settled and we wouldn't be drifting into any other boats while we crabbed. Phoebe scurried to begin unwinding the crab lines, which are nothing more than a metal hook on the end of a string. The bait would be attached to the hook and lowered into the water. When the crab was busy hanging on and enjoying the meal, we would just lift the string slowly until the crab came into view just below the water's surface, and then we'd swoop the net under it. And just like that, we'd have ourselves a crab. It seemed almost too simple, but it worked. Crabs aren't very smart, and I guess they didn't realize that what they'd been eating was being dropped down from above and then pulled back up again. Hey, whatever works, I guess.

"Casey, get over here and put the bait on," Phoebe yelled to me. "You know I'm not touching this stuff!"

"Aww, come on, Phoebes!" Nick took a frozen dead fish and waved it in her face. "If we don't catch any crabs, we'll fry one of these bunkers up instead!" Phoebe screamed and jumped away as Nick and Zack laughed at her reaction.

"Idiots!" She yelled back at them, pouting, and settling herself onto one of the seats in the boat. She was under protest now, and wouldn't help set up the rest of the lines. Nick, Zack and I picked up the slack, and before you knew it there were ten lines in the water attached to the sides of the boat, five with chicken legs, and five with bunker. We settled back to let the lines soak for a few minutes, and our conversation fell to school. Nick mentioned that he couldn't wait to see Matt in September to see what the fallout was from the party. He had heard that Matt's parents were going to be renting out the house here at the Cove for the rest of the summer, and he wondered if it was because of Matt's big party this past weekend.

"I heard that there were over a hundred kids there at one point," Nick said. "My dad would have freaked if that had been my house."

"Mine, too. Can you imagine having that party with Pauley living next door? No way that would ever happen!" I added.

"My parents would freak, no doubt about it," Phoebe said, as she twirled her hair and tried to stay far away from any of the chicken pieces that were left over and sitting on the floor beneath her feet. "What ever happened with that Mike kid? Zack sure took him for a ride!"

"He better never set foot near me," Zack growled, teeth clenched. "Or near you." He reached out and touched my knee as I sat opposite him. I looked at him and smiled. He smiled back and then lifted his face with eyes closed to take in the sun while we sat and waited for the crabs to bite. I looked at him while his eyes were closed as he basked in the warmth of the sun's rays and examined his perfect features. His long eyelashes and perfectly shaped nose. His lips, soft but not feminine, and he had just a bit of stubble on his chin — not yet enough to grow a beard, but enough to know that he would someday. The curls in his hair sat just above his eyebrows, and showed a hint of light highlights from his time in the salt water since he'd arrived here. His skin, now glowing the color of honey, looked healthy. Yes, he was yummy. A sharp elbow in my side broke my concentration as Phoebe got my attention. She gave me a look that told me she knew where my mind was, and her smile said she approved. I giggled at her.

"What's so funny?" Zack asked, as he picked up his head and focused his big brown eyes on me.

"Nothing. Phoebe. She's . . . funny." I stammered back at him, glancing at Phoebe with a scowl to let her know that we had just been caught, and I wasn't happy about it.

Nick decided it was time to check the lines to see if any crabs were finding our bunker and chicken legs appetizing. He grabbed the long-handled net and settled himself next to one of the lines and called Zack over for a lesson in nabbing a crab. Zack jumped out of his seat, anxious to learn the technique, and positioned himself next to Nick's side.

"First, you lightly pull the line towards you until it's tight, and you'll feel a slight tugging if there is something nibbling on your bait." He demonstrated for Zack exactly what he meant. "This one has something on it, so take the line and feel it. Do you feel the slight tugging? He's pulling the bait off with his claw."

"I don't understand how we pull him up though. Won't he realize that his dinner is moving away from him?"

"No," Nick explained. "Because of the current in the water, the crabs hold on with one claw, and pull off the pieces of meat with the other. Since the water's always moving, they know instinctively to keep a tight hold of whatever they are eating. So they'll hold on for the entire time you are pulling them closer to the boat."

"Okay, so do I just start pulling him in now?"

"Yes." Nick continued with his lesson. "No jerky movements, just slow and steady. If the crab is busy eating, he'll hold on the whole way." Zack continued to pull the string, letting it fall in a small pile into the boat, using two hands and alternating in a steady movement as the bait began to move closer to us. It wasn't long before the murky water gave way to the sight of a floating crab, just below the surface of the water, grasping onto a chicken leg. "Now, don't let the chicken break the surface of the water. Keep it steady while I scoop it. Hold it right there, Zack." Nick took the net and positioned it just behind the crab and swept it through the water slowly from behind, dipped below the bait and lifted both it and the crab right out of the water. A perfect net job! Zack was thrilled.

"Holy Cow! That is so cool! Look at that thing! My first crab! Get my camera. I want a picture of this." Zack was so giddy with excitement that we all felt it too. Nick handed him the net to hold while he reached in and grabbed the crab from behind, being cautious of the two rather large claws, and lifted it from the netting. He held it in front of Zack as they posed for a photo.

"Now we keep doing that to all of the lines?" Zack was pumped up and enjoying this immensely. His smile was ear to ear, and I found myself smiling along with him. His smile was so contagious.

"Yup, just keep going. When you feel that you have one, just yell 'NET' and someone will grab it and net it for you." Nick walked the crab he was holding over to the bucket and dropped it in, but not before taking a quick measurement on the ruler he had mounted to the side of the console. "Six inches. That's a good one, Zack!" The crab skidded along the bottom of the bucket trying to regain its composure after his afternoon meal had been so rudely interrupted by the intrusion of our net.

Zack worked his way around both sides of the boat, checking lines, yelling for a net, doing what he was taught as he pulled the strings and continued to bring in crab after crab after crab. Phoebe and I just watched and enjoyed the sight of Zack making a killing of the day's catch. "My dad's going to love making crab gravy for tonight's pasta," Nick said. Zack smiled and continued working the lines while Phoebe and I snapped a few more pictures of him.

After about two hours, Zack had managed to pull in about three dozen crabs — enough for the pasta gravy and to have a few on the side as well. All in all, it was a great day spent crabbing on the bay. We decided to end this activity and head into town for some pizza. Nick pulled the lines in with Zack and dropped the bait back into the bay, while Phoebe and I were in charge of rolling up the lines so they wouldn't tangle and then storing them away. We used the hand sanitizer that I always brought along on our crabbing trips to clean up a bit. I pulled up the anchor so we could get underway. Phoebe stood with Nick at the center console while he drove us back in, and Zack and I snuggled on the stern seat. Zack was still smiling, excited about his catch today, his one arm around my shoulder, the other holding my hand in his lap. I rested my head on his shoulder, thinking about how this would be the last time I'd get to do this with him this summer, or maybe forever. It made me sad.

I was dreading tonight's shift at the Polar Palace. After a great afternoon crabbing and sharing pizza with Zack, Nick and Phoebe, I had to get home, shower and then head into work. Tonight's shift started early, at five instead of six, and would go until ten o'clock. The only good thing about it was that Zack was going to meet me after work, and we were going to hang out together since he was leaving tomorrow. We secretly planned on staying out very late and selfishly weren't going to have Nick and Phoebe around. We wanted to spend this last night alone without them. I felt bad about ditching Phoebe, but Zack said that he'd tell Nick to plan something with her that didn't include us. Then he'd be the bad guy and not me. I was cool with that plan.

"I'm not going to be able to hang out tonight, Case. Nick has something special planned for me. I'm so excited! I hope you don't mind."

"Wow, that's great, Phoebes. I can't wait to hear all about it tomorrow!" I played along with the game, secretly letting out a sigh of relief that I wouldn't have to be the one to ditch her. "What do you think it is?"

"I bet it's a moonlight cruise around the bay. I always wanted to do that with him. I kept dropping hints, so maybe that's it! How romantic! And there's a full moon tonight!"

"Fill me in tomorrow, Phoebes. I want to hear every detail."

"What are you and Zack doing?"

"I think we'll get some pizza and then take a walk. It's his last night, so . . . just hanging." I didn't want Phoebe to know that Zack and I planned to hang out behind the upside down lifeguard stand tonight. Hopefully Pauley wouldn't be snooping around there either. Not that anything might be going on, but I would have liked to have had my privacy tonight. It would be bad enough tomorrow when I had to recount every detail for her. Come to think of it, I had better take some good notes tonight.

Right on time; the bells above the door jingled at 9:55 to let us know that someone had come in. This time it wasn't a customer, but Nick and Zack. Zack had a blanket tucked under his arm, and a big smile on his face. "Hey, Gorgeous, you almost ready?"

My heart melted. How had I come to feel so much for this boy in less than two weeks? My stomach fluttered now whenever I caught sight of him. In fact, the mere mention of his name made me jittery. What happened to me? And now, this was his last night here. I wanted him to remember it. To remember me. I wanted to remember him. I touched my wrist where I wore the charm bracelet he had given me. I made sure to wear it tonight to show him how much I loved it, and how much I cared about him. "I just need to wash up and restock. Just a couple of minutes," I sang to him with a smile.

He plopped into one of the seats, and Phoebe locked the door while we closed up shop. Then we all left together, Phoebe and Nick headed toward the bay on their bikes after a quick goodbye, while Zack and I headed the other way, up to the ocean. Knowing that our bikes would be a dead giveaway to the Bike Cops if they were in the bike rack at the boardwalk, we left the bikes down at the Polar Palace. We figured we'd pick them up there on the way home.

As usual, the boardwalk was quiet. My stomach did somersaults as we walked hand-in-hand over to the dune opening. Zack took charge, and led us onto the beach. This time, we didn't leave our flip flops at the opening; instead, we brought them with us. We didn't want anything to bring attention to the fact that we were up here tonight. Zack dropped my hand only when he was ready to lay the blanket out on the sand. He picked a quiet spot behind the lifeguard stand, out of view of anyone walking onto the beach to peek at the moon or watch the waves in the moonlight. He wanted seclusion. Tonight it would just be Zack and me.

"This looks like a good spot. Okay?" He asked me as one eyebrow lifted slightly on his brow. "We can still see the moon, but no one would really be able to see us here."

"It's perfect," I whispered, and sank my knees into the soft plush of the blanket and the sand beneath it. Zack positioned himself next to me — his back leaning against the wood of the stand, knees bent. He opened his legs and patted the blanket as an invitation to me to sit between them, and I did. Leaning back against his chest and propping my hands on his knees, we both just sat in silence enjoying our beautiful view of the dark ocean and the black sky with a beautiful white moon glimmering over it. The waves crashed to shore providing a beautiful music, Mother Nature's finest concert for sure. It was the perfect setting for us to share our last hours together before my life returned to what used to be normal in Cranberry Cove.

"Did you enjoy your crab dinner tonight?" I asked Zack to break the quiet. I was beginning to get hypnotized by his rhythmic breathing behind me.

"It was delicious, actually. Nick's dad is a great cook. We had pasta and sauce, and he grilled a few crabs with some seasoning and he showed me how to pick out the meat from the claws. We pigged out."

"Well, I'm glad you liked them. You sure did all the work to get them!"

"It was fun. Nick said next time I come, we'll go again. The pictures turned out great. Did you see them?"

"Yeah, Phoebe and I were looking at them at work. We'll have to post some online." Another pause in the conversation, and I felt Zack's hand begin to move up over my arm in a sweet caress, and then around my middle as he held me in place. I dropped my hands from his knees and interlaced my fingers in his as they rested on my stomach. Zack lowered his face next to mine and kissed my neck softly.

"I wish I wasn't leaving tomorrow. I'm glad I got to spend two weeks here, but it went so fast."

"I know what you mean. It flew by. I'm going to miss you." Zack pulled me back into his chest, as if he didn't want to let go. I felt the same.

"Casey, I want to tell you about myself. I'm not such a nice guy. I've had a tough time growing up, what with my parent's divorce and all. I did things that weren't nice. I got into trouble." He pulled me around so I could look at him as he continued. "I have a record. I went to juvie and I have a record. I stole stuff, and broke into buildings." I just sat quietly as he spoke, knowing that this was his confession to me, and he needed to get things out in the open before he left tomorrow. He wanted me to know who he was, and I wanted to know too, so I let him keep going and didn't interrupt. He took a breath and tried to find the right words. "I got kicked out of my old school. That's how bad it was. My mom was forced to move so I could go to a new school. I got a fresh start. I wanted to do better, but the kids I hung with were bad and not good role models. Then I met Nick at my new school, on the first day. His locker was next to mine, and he just started talking to me. He knew nothing about me, but just started to talk to me, and that was it. We clicked, you know? He's a great kid. He introduced me to some nice kids and he made sure I always knew what was assigned for homework, and he kept me busy. I owe my new start in life to Nick, a kid I never knew before, and yet he saved my life. And then he introduced me to you, and my life changed again."

"Zack, that's such a nice thing to say."

"Wait, let me finish." I closed my mouth, respecting that there was more that he needed to say. He grabbed both my hands in his and held them up between us, looking me right in the eyes. "I've been with a few girls, not in a good way. I made them do things they probably regretted. I know I regret it. I was reckless and didn't care. Now I care. I care a lot. I want you to know that the old me would have taken advantage of you badly. I would have not cared about it at all. But the new me, well, I see how perfect and sweet and beautiful you are and I can't ever imagine hurting you or disrespecting you like that — I just want you to know that. You are so special to me, Casey, and I'll never be able to go back to the old me again. I don't think I'll ever be able to find a girl who makes my heart feel the way you make it feel. I never cared about a girl before, Casey, except for the five minutes I was all over her. But you changed that. And that's what I wanted to say to you." He settled back and turned me around to lean back into him, while I tried to absorb what his words meant. It was obviously a confession he needed to make to me. His sigh of relief when he was done was an indication of the weight that was lifted from his shoulders. His arms once again wrapped around me, and I felt his slow, steady breathing commence again.

I felt I needed to say something to him, but the words just weren't there. I couldn't get anything to come from my head and through my lips, so I spun around and took his face in my hands, one on either side of his cheeks. I looked him in the eye — those big brown eyes, and leaned closer and kissed him. For a few seconds, he didn't know what to make of it, and he didn't know what to do with his arms. They sort of just hung there, as if his brain didn't register what was happening. But then he wrapped them around me and pulled me closer to him, wrapping me in himself, his softness, his chest, cradling me and kissing me back. I held his face, and when I pulled away from that kiss, I saw in his eyes a warmth and affection that I've never known before in my life. His connection to me at that moment was so honest; we had given ourselves to each other silently in that kiss. Zack was mine. And I was his.

No other words were spoken that night between us. Just kissing and cuddling, fingers laced together, thumbs stroking over the charms of my beautiful bracelet that he'd given me. Never once did I feel that Zack would take me to a place I wasn't ready to visit. Never did I feel nervous with him. His declaration of his feelings for me, his respect for me, put me at ease and allowed me to enjoy Zack and his love for me for hours. He was as surprised as I was when over the horizon we noticed that the black sky was beginning to show signs of pink.

"It's predawn. The sun's going to be rising soon. We've been here all night." Zack pulled me closer yet again, making no effort to get up, an indication to me that we would be enjoying our first sunrise together in just a little while.

"Are you going to be in trouble for being out all night?" Zack asked in my ear.

"I told my mom I'd probably be staying at Phoebe's house, so I'll text Phoebe to make sure she doesn't stop over until I'm home."

"I don't like you lying to your mom, but I'm glad you did. This was a night I'll never forget."

"I won't either. I . . . I love you, Zack."

"I love you, too, Casey."

Watching the sun rise while in Zack's arms was a scene I'd be playing over and over in my head forever. Watching the car pull away that would be taking him back up north is something I'd like to forget. It was heartbreaking to say the least. No, that's not a strong enough word. It was as if my heart was being ripped from my chest. I'd managed to hold back my tears, but once I snuck into Nick's room with Phoebe, I let it all out.

"You okay, Casey? Can I get you anything?" I was hunched over Nick's dresser, my head buried in my arms, my chest heaving and weeping making it difficult to breathe.

"Why am I crying like this? This isn't me. It's crazy! I can't control myself!" I picked up my head and looked at her. Nick wasn't in the room. I'll thank him later for allowing me some dignity and not being there when I fell apart. Phoebe just looked at me sympathetically, and used her thumbs to wipe the wetness from my cheeks. She grabbed a tissue from the bedside table and offered it to me, and I accepted.

"You love him, that's why. You watched the guy who stole your heart drive away with it. What do you expect to happen?"

"I need to get over this quickly. I can't get through the day falling apart like this. We need to do something today. Beach?" Phoebe nodded in agreement, her hands rubbed my arms in support. I took a deep cleansing breath in an effort to pull myself back into a more presentable state, and pulled her into a hug. "Thank you for being here for me. I owe you one."

"Don't worry about it. That's what best friends are for. You better make sure you are here for me the day Nick leaves."

"Definitely. You can count on it." Another hug, and then we headed out of Nick's bedroom and into the living room where Nick sat patiently waiting for us.

"You okay, Casey?" Nick asked. "I just got a text from Zack asking me how you are."

"I'm okay, just sad. How's Zack?"

"Same as you. See?" He shoved his phone in front of me so I could read the text from Zack:

Zack: I miss her already. Pls check on her. Tell her I left my heart in Cranberry Cove.

When I went through the back door of my house, I noticed Sasha giving me the "you've been neglecting me" look. She wanted to get some exercise, so I leashed her up and gathered her tennis balls to get her ready for a romp at the ball field. Sasha loved seeing her dog friends there, especially the Golden Retriever named Mya and the Brussels Griffon named Zoey. A note on the kitchen table from my mom mentioned that her errands this morning would keep her out most of the day — for that I was grateful. I didn't want her asking me how I was now that Zack was gone. It was just too soon to open up that wound right now. Hopefully, by later this afternoon, it would have scabbed over a bit and I'd be able to mention his name without breaking down. I texted Phoebe that I'd be ready for the beach in about an hour. Sasha and I headed down the street, my face hidden behind dark sunglasses to hide the fact that I'd been crying. I didn't need the neighbors to make any inquiries this morning.

The time at the ball field with Sasha gave me a chance to pull myself together. In my mind, I was able to talk myself back into a better state of mind, and focus on the great time I had over the last two weeks with Zack; not just on the sorrow I felt over the loss of this morning. I vowed to myself that I would wear his bracelet all the time as a reminder of my first summer love, and knowing I could text him the rest of the summer and share in his new adventures while he was visiting upstate New York and Florida made me feel a bit more connected to him. I left the ball field in a better state of mind than when I arrived, feeling hopeful that my friendship with Zack might be able to sustain over the months ahead. Sasha left feeling absolutely exhausted after romping around for an hour with Mya and Zoey.

Phoebe met me at my house and waited while I put on my one-piece suit and gathered my beach bag. I had checked the water conditions on the way to the ball field and saw that the tide was perfect for some bodysurfing. I had recently started a new novel, and looked forward to getting lost in someone else's tragic love story as a means to forget about my own for a while. We mounted our bikes and headed up for some much-needed diversion by means of some hot lifeguards and rocking waves.

Our usual spot behind the lifeguard stand (and Jase) was open, so we nabbed it and set up shop. Phoebe immediately got lost in her celebrity gossip magazines, but I set my sights on some eye candy, as in Phoebe's brother. A quick scan of the area verified the absence of one Blondie Sarah, and somehow that gave me a sense of relief. I wasn't in the mood to watch anyone swooning over a guy today, unless of course it was me.

I decided to pay Jase a little visit, thinking it might distract me from Zack. No luck. "Ummm, excuse me, Mr. Lifeguard, do you know the water temperature?"

"Yeah, it's seventy-five." He never looked down to see it was me. I kept going.

"Umm, Mr. Lifeguard, do you know if there are any sharks in the water?"

"No, no sharks here." He still didn't look down. What the heck? Time to bring out the big guns.

"Umm, Mr. Lifeguard, you sure have some big muscles!" With that, his head flew over the side of the stand and gaped at me.

"Beach Girl! What's up? You got me good on that one!" He chuckled and pushed the hair from his eyes with a swipe of his hand. Man, he looked good up on that pedestal.

"I heard Zack left this morning."

How did he know that? "Yeah, his mom picked him up. How'd you know?"

"I asked, I mean, Phoebe told me." He looked back out to the water, and then as if he was trying to change the subject, for which I was glad, he added, "The water looks great for bodysurfing today. You going in?"

"Yeah, I'm thinking about it."

"Well, I'm due for a break in about ten minutes. Wait for me and I'll go with you." I must have had the dumbest look on my face, because I didn't answer, and I didn't blink. I just kind of stared. Did he just say he wanted to go in the water . . . with me? "Casey, you'll wait for me? I'll come get you. Okay?"

"Uh, yeah, cool. I'll be there." I stumbled away, walking quickly before he could change his mind. Wow. Swimming with Jase! How cool is that? I plopped back into my chair and wouldn't look in his direction. I just picked up my book from my beach bag and opened it up. Phoebe looked at me like I had two heads.

"How's the book?"

"Good. Good book."

"Easy to read?"

"Not bad."

"You're very talented."

"Really? Why?"

"Because you're holding the book upside down, you doofus! What the heck has gotten into you?"

"Oh, ahh, nothing. I'm going to go body surfing in a little bit. Just going to read a while and then go. Good waves. Good to go bodysurfing." I quickly flipped the book around. She must have thought I was nuts the way I was babbling on, but my brain was just so scattered. Phoebe would have died if she knew that Jase was putting me in a tizzy like this. What had gotten into me this summer? It's as if Zack unleashed all kinds of emotions inside of me and now I was just a body full of crazy. I kept my eyes on the print of the page in front of me and hid my face behind the book. She reached over and pushed the book down so she could see me.

"Really, Casey, are you okay? I mean, you were pretty upset this morning. I'm just worried about you."

I sighed, and put my book down into my lap and threw my head back. "Ugh! I have no idea if I'm okay or not. The past two weeks have been crazy, nothing that I could have ever imagined, and now he's gone and I'm expected to go back to normal. What is normal, anyway? Am I supposed to just forget all about him? Act as if he doesn't exist anymore? Go on with my life?"

"How did you leave things with him? Are you seeing other people?"

"Seeing other people? What other people? How can anyone compare to him? He's like . . . like . . . well, I have nothing to compare him with because I've never kissed a guy before him! We didn't even talk about seeing anyone, or each other again, because he's off now visiting relatives for the rest of the summer!" I put my hands over my face and pulled them slowly downward, making eye contact with Phoebe as she just sat quietly, listening to me ramble. "I need to find a way to not dwell on him. I have to accept that this was the best two weeks of my life, and move on. Right? I need to move on, right Phoebes?"

Phoebe just shrugged her shoulders. "I guess so," she said. "I don't know what to tell you, Casey. When I talk to Nick later, I'll see if Zack mentioned anything to him. Have you texted him since he left?"

"No, I just figured he'd text me if he wanted to talk. I don't think I want to text him. Should I?"

"I don't know, why not? Just find out how his trip home went. Tell him you had a great time with him. Wish him a safe trip to New York State. Just say anything."

I thought about it a minute, and tried to get my nerve up to actually do it. What's the worst that can happen? I grabbed my phone out of my bag and looked at her. "Should I do it?" I waited for a response from her, but was interrupted by someone grabbing my shoulders from behind me.

"Ready to hit the waves, Casey? I'm on my break. Let's go in!" I turned to see Jase, looking all tan and buff and gorgeous standing behind me in his red Cranberry Cove lifeguard trunks, which were hanging just perfectly on his hips. I looked back at Phoebe as I tossed my phone back into my bag.

"Phoebes, I'm diving back in — head first. We'll finish the conversation later." Jase extended his hand to me to help pull me out of my chair, and off we went, down the beach and into the water.

"So, where's Sarah?" I asked him once we got out to the spot where the waves just begin to take shape. We were surrounded with ladies floating around in their flowered bathing caps and a few other swimmers eagerly awaiting the next big one to form.

"She's shopping today with her friends. Taking a break from the beach."

"Oh." I didn't really know what else to say, and his response basically answered my question. At least I knew I didn't have to worry about watching that spectacle play out in front of the lifeguard stand again today. Of course there would probably be others, but somehow I felt Sarah was staking claim and getting pretty well settled in as a first-stringer in this game with Jase. "Will she be going home soon?"

"Home?" He chuckled when he said it. "No, she's staying the rest of the summer. Why do you ask? I didn't think you liked her."

"Why would you think that?" I questioned. "I don't even know her!"

"Exactly! I tried to introduce you that night at the party and you refused. So why the sudden interest in her now?" I thought he was teasing me. I thought he knew exactly why I was asking and wanted me to say it. I would not be telling him the real reason, no way, no how.

"I just wasn't in the mood right then. I needed to find Nick and Phoebe." I said matter-of-factly and then dipped underwater so he wouldn't keep asking me my intentions for asking about her. When I came up and wiped my face, he was still looking at me with a smirk, and I knew he knew. "Beach Girl, you're cute when you're jealous." He then dipped under the water, leaving me bobbing there with my mouth wide open. He emerged and shook his head, spraying me with the water that flew from his hair. "Let's catch some waves, Beach Girl. Show me what you've got." And just like that, our conversation was over, and I was left hanging trying to figure out what to make of it.

Luckily, a wave began to form just beyond where we were waiting. We watched it for a few seconds and knew that this would be one neither of us wanted to miss. We positioned ourselves, along with the others, but away from the floating bathing cap ladies, and began to swim in time to be lifted and taken by the wave and hurtled towards shore. We both rode it masterfully, dodging kids and adults in our way, head to head with each other as the water splashed around us, until we were grounded in the sand and shells at the water's edge. Sputtering for air, we both rolled around in the shallow water until it retreated and beached us. I quickly checked the girls and found they were in need of some assistance, springing free of their fabric, but I was able to adjust quickly without anyone seeing.

"Great ride, Beach Girl! You do it better than anyone!" He laughed at me as he struggled to his feet; adjusting his own suit just a bit. "Let's go again!"

So I jumped up and together we headed out again for another round. *Take that, Blondie!*

"Have you heard from Zack yet?" Nick quizzed me as we sat in Phoebe's back yard, waiting for her to apply some finishing touches to her hair, which always looked perfect even if she didn't comb it. I kicked a few stones with my feet.

"Nah, nothing yet. I texted him a few times, but never heard back." I had sent texts twice in the three days since he'd left — carefully worded texts that just asked how he was and if he was enjoying his vacation with his mom and family in New York.

"Me neither. It's not like him not to text back. I wonder what's up?"

"I don't know," I mumbled as I played with the charms on my charm bracelet, allowing each one I touched to take me back to the special time with him it represented. "Maybe he's just really busy, or his phone died or something. I'm sure we'll eventually hear from him."

Our conversation ended as Phoebe emerged from the back door, giving us a "TA-DAH!" and a twirl to show us her new shirt and her perfectly done hair. Mine was thrown back into a ponytail, my usual summer do. No muss, no fuss. Nick responded first. "Looks beautiful,

Phoebe, NOW can we get going?" I'm glad he emphasized the NOW part, because if he didn't, I sure was going to do it. We were biking to the amusement pier in the town south of us to walk the boardwalk and jump on the new rollercoaster. The pier would no doubt be packed tonight since it's the start of the weekend, but that's what made it fun. The more crowded, the more people watching you can do. You never know what crazy people you'll see on the pier at night.

"I'm ready! I'm looking forward to a meatball sandwich and some zeppoles! I hope they are good and greasy tonight." Phoebe led us out her back gate and to our bikes which were sitting in the driveway. "We are all riding the Merry-Go-Round tonight. Casey, don't say a word. You are riding it, and you will enjoy it!" She knew it was my least favorite thing to do there. She always wanted to sit on one of those horses that had a cute name like Patsy or Daisy, and it would rise up and down the entire ride while we watched parents blowing kisses and waving to their kids on the ride, all the while listening to organ music replaying the same song over and over and over. Yeesh. I always tried to avoid it and use that time to excuse myself to use the ladies' room. I guessed I wouldn't be able to get out of it this time.

The bike ride to the amusement pier took about fifteen minutes. Since we weren't in Cranberry Cove, we always made sure to bring a bike lock to lock our bikes together. It was the only time we locked up all summer. The town where the pier was located was much bigger than the Cove, and catered to a wilder crowd. It would be best we all stayed together while we wandered around tonight.

There was such a sense of freedom that came with living on the island, because so many of the businesses catered to teens, it was as if the entire island was a playground. The amusement pier played host to many families. However, the majority of the visitors were teenagers running free, eating junk food and playing the many stands, trying to win a stuffed animal for a sweetheart or a t-shirt featuring their favorite band. Visitors from all over came here, and Phoebe and I loved to figure out where people came from based on how they dressed and how they spoke. People with New York accents were easy to figure out, and so were those who came from the Philadelphia area. Even the North Jersey people were easy to pick out. It became somewhat of a game for us as we picked a bench and ate our frozen custard or munched on French fries, just watching the groups of people walk by while the sound of the ocean waves crashing to shore hummed behind us.

We made our way up the boardwalk ramp after we locked our bikes in one of the many racks located at the street ends. As we had assumed, the place was already packed, although the sun had just set about a half hour earlier. The place really came alive once darkness set in, highlighting the many neon and flashing signs that littered the buildings along the boardwalk and pier. Our first stop was the ticket booth. We wanted to get onto the roller coaster before we ate anything, just to make sure that whatever we did eat stayed with us and didn't end up in the Atlantic Ocean. We all had a bad experience once when we ate early and then jumped on a ride that just went in circles at really high speed. While the ride was great, our pizza and soda didn't enjoy it so much, and we never wanted to repeat that scene ever again.

With tickets in hand, we headed over to the line that was forming for the new roller coaster which was called "The Reaper." Nick and Phoebe held hands, albeit discreetly, but I still felt like the third wheel. I guess I should just get used to it since Phoebe and Nick still had half a summer to spend together. Luckily, a vibration in my back pocket distracted me from feeling sad and I dug my phone out and checked the message.

Zack: Hey Miss You!

It was from Zack! A huge smile spread across my face as Nick reached into his pocket and took out his vibrating phone as well. Finally, Zack responded to our texts. I texted back.

Text between Casey and Zack:

Casey: Hi! We r at the pier waiting to get on the roller coaster. Miss you too!

Zack: Phone died. Had to get new cable. Left mine at Nick's. Sorry.

Casey: no prob. Glad you are OK. Having fun?

Zack: So far. Not as much as at the beach. Nick with you?

Casey: Yes, he just got your txt. Responding now.

Zack: Wish I was there!

Casey: Me too.

Well, that made me feel better. Just knowing Zack was thinking of me made me happy. Nick was still texting with him as we moved forward in the line, and it wasn't long before we were getting loaded into one of the cars of the roller coaster. With feet dangling free, the three of us waited for that first jerky movement forward. It signaled we were now committed to making it through the loops and dips that would take us over the Atlantic Ocean and (hopefully) safely back to the pier again. The final check by the ride attendant to ensure our harnesses were secure seemed to go without a hitch, and a thumbs up signaled to the operator in the booth set the ride in motion. It didn't disappoint, and after enduring Phoebe's screams in my ear for the thirty-four point seven seconds we were moving. We were returned virtually unscathed back to our starting point. Our stomachs, on the other hand, not so unscathed. The loops and dips certainly took their toll and we all agreed we'd need to wait a bit before seeking out the meatball sandwiches and French fries.

"So, what's Zack up to tonight?" I asked Nick as we settled into a bench along the boardwalk to start the people watching part of our evening.

"Going to a party with his cousins," Nick replied. "He has one cousin about our age, and another that's seventeen. They're a bit wild, but Zack gets along pretty well with them. I told him to text us later."

"Oh, okay." I wasn't sure how I felt about Zack going to a party. If it was anything like the party we went to at Matt's house, then he could be around alcohol, girls and drugs. With Zack's background, that was probably not a good place for him to be. It made me a bit uneasy. Nick took note of my quiet mood and nudged me with his elbow.

"I know what you're thinking, Casey, but you can't worry about Zack. Anything he does now is his own choice, and we have to just hope that he'll make good choices."

"Did he, ummm, say anything to you about me, you know, before he left?" I didn't really know how to ask or even what I was asking of Nick, so I just blurted it out the best I could. "I'm not sure how we really ended it the other day."

"Zack had a great time with you. You touched something in him. I never saw him like that before. You definitely touched him in some way. I hope that next summer we can all be together again. You guys were really perfect together. Don't you feel that way, Casey?"

"I do, Nick. I really, really like him. I hope I do get to see him again."

"Umm, are you two done whispering to each other so we can start enjoying the scenery? I need some help here! There were three families that already passed by and I couldn't identify their accents!" Phoebe yelled at us from the other end of the bench, a bit out of sorts since we didn't include her in the conversation. So, we settled back and began to watch the people who walked by until our stomachs were ready to take in some dinner.

People watching now behind us, Nick was the first to stand up and announce that his stomach was ready to enjoy some meatballs. The best meatball sandwiches can be found at a stand that sits in the middle of the boardwalk, and always boasts a long line no matter what time of day or night. We strolled in that direction, but Phoebe needed to use the restroom before we sat down to eat, so a quick stop off at the arcade would take care of that. While Phoebe went into the bathroom, Nick threw a few quarters in one of the game machines to keep busy. I decided to wander through the rows of machines, eyeing up the latest games and enjoying the sights and sounds of the arcade. My eyes caught sight of some very nice looking guys, huddled around a pinball machine. One of them had a girl hanging off of him as he worked the flippers and pushed against the machine, racking up points while the others around him watched and cheered him on. Something about the girl made me move a bit closer to get a better look. There was something familiar about her, but I couldn't quite place her. I needed a better look at her, so I crept around to another aisle near the skeeball machines so I could get a better angle. What I saw stopped me dead in my tracks. It was her! It was Blondie Sarah, and she was hanging all over the hottie who was flipping and pushing and riding that pinball game like he was in a rodeo. I felt my bottom jaw hit the floor. What was this? Why was she hanging on this guy? WHO WAS THIS GUY?

"Ooooh, Kyle, you are the best pinball player!" I heard her croon as she pushed the blonde hair out of her face and twirled the edges around her finger. Her cropped t-shirt showed off her tanned stomach. *Is that a navel piercing?* Her short-shorts accentuated her long legs. She once again wore too much makeup, but something told me that this Kyle kid probably wasn't spending much time looking at her face — her other body parts were far too appealing.

"Thanks, Babe," he responded, smacking his gum but never once taking his eyes off the game. "After this, let's go take a ride on the Reaper!"

"Only if you hold my hand the whole time, Kyle. You know how scared I am of heights!" She pouted although it was lost on him since he never looked away from the tiny metal ball that clanged its way through the maze of the game.

"Of course, Baby, I'll hold you so tight, don't worry about it." He turned his head to her and quickly gave her a wink and a smile, and then his eyes went back to the game. I stood motionless, not wanting to be seen by her, but I couldn't pull myself away. So many questions still rattled around inside my head. Why was she not with Jase? I looked back towards where Nick was playing his game. Still no sign of Phoebe. I had to ask her if Jase broke up with Sarah. I needed to know because there was no way I'd let Sarah break his heart by cheating on him with this guy, which is exactly what I suspected was going on. Jase was too good to deserve that kind of treatment. I hurriedly walked back towards Nick, just as Phoebe emerged from the bathroom.

"Phoebes! Get over here! I whispered loudly over the sounds of the arcade, frantically waving my hand to get her attention. "Come over here!" She saw me and gave me a quizzical look but then made her way over to me with some speed.

"What? Why are you whispering?" she asked me, looking around but not knowing what she should be looking for.

"Where is Jase?"

"What? What do you want him for?"

"I just want to know where he is!" I continued to whisper-yell, my frustration evident in my body language as I tried to get her to just answer my question and not question why.

"Home, I guess. I don't know. Why?" I could tell she was getting annoyed at me, and didn't want to waste her time with a conversation that centered around her brother.

"Come with me!" I dragged her by the arm back to the aisle by the skeeball machines to give her a look at what I saw. "Look! Look who's over there. At the pinball machine." I whispered to her, pulling her body into position so she would look in the right direction.

"What? What am I looking at?" she whispered over her shoulder to me, since I was hiding behind her, her eyes frantically searching the area in front of her but still not knowing what she should be looking for.

"Blondie! Who is she with? Did Jase break up with her?" She stilled, and I could tell her eyes now focused on our target.

"I don't know! I don't keep track of his stupid love life!" I continued to hide behind her, keeping my eyes on Sarah and her mystery man. "This is stupid and I'm hungry. Let's go eat already!" She turned on her heel and headed back to Nick.

I caught up with her and jumped in her path, my hands folded in front of her pleading, "You have to text him. Find out if they broke up. Please, Phoebes, please? For me? Please?" I begged her, showing no shame in my display.

"What? You text him! I can't ask him that!" She shook her head at me and grabbed my shoulders. "What is going on with you? Why do you care?" She looked me in the eye. I couldn't answer. I just stared at her. Her face softened as she finally realized what my motivation was. "Oh, no," she said quietly, "you like him, don't you? Oh, Casey, don't tell me you like my brother! I thought it was just a friendly crush! You aren't serious!" I could tell that my silence was confirming what she was now just coming to realize.

"I just don't want him to get hurt! If you don't text him, then I'm going to find out from Sarah what she's doing with that kid!"

"Are you nuts? What are you planning to do?" Her hands still held my shoulders, but gripped tighter now, her fingernails most likely making indents in my skin as she tried to assess the seriousness of my last outburst. "You can't go over there and just ask her! You'll look like a doofus!"

She was right. I needed a way to get in front of her casually and then happen to mention Jase to see what her reaction would be. I took another look over in Sarah's direction. The pinball machine was silent — they must have finished the game and moved on. "Come with me!" I dragged her by the hand and began to frantically search the arcade, pulling her behind me, dragging her as we weaved our way through the crowds of gamers and families. Then I saw her, standing in line at the refreshment stand, hand-in-hand with that Kyle kid, and twirling her hair around her finger with the other. I stopped dead in my tracks, causing Phoebe to run into me and almost knock me down like a bowling pin. "There she is! I'm going in!" I started to move towards them as they stood in line whispering to each other, pointing at the menu items listed on signs that hung over their heads.

"Wait!" Phoebe grabbed my arm and held me back. "What are you going to say?"

"I don't know, but I have to go now before I lose sight of them again!" I took a deep breath and walked with purpose over to the refreshment stand line, hoping that by the time I reached Sarah the right words would appear on my tongue. Phoebe followed behind, and I was glad she did. I figured that Sarah would probably recognize Phoebe as being Jase's sister and that would help me keep her off balance. I positioned myself right beside her, as if I just happened to walk by and noticed her.

"Oh, it's . . . Sarah, right?" I snapped my fingers, playing as if I was trying to remember her name, as if I vaguely recognized her from somewhere. She turned her head quickly to me, and once she had placed me, I saw her eyes widen and her face lose some color. I continued on, not giving her a chance to respond. "I think I saw you at the beach in the Cove, and at a party . . . with Jase, right?" I played dumb, putting on my best thinking-face, as if I was really trying to figure this out.

"Umm, yeah," she stammered back, casually dropping her hand from Kyle's causing him to suddenly become interested in the conversation. Phoebe just stood behind me, but then finally piped in to help. She moved slightly forward towards Sarah so that her voice could be heard over the noises from the arcade games.

"Is my brother here tonight?" Phoebe moved her head from side to side, as if searching for him. "I needed to ask him something." Phoebe spoke over my shoulder to Sarah, giving a look that I wish I had a camera to capture. It was one of those 'you are so caught right now, sister!' looks.

"Ah, no, he isn't here right now," she replied quietly, trying to turn her back and dismiss us to end the conversation, but I wasn't finished with her yet. Time to come in for the kill.

"Who's your friend?" I asked her, pointing my thumb at him. She ignored me, hoping, I'm sure, that the floor would swallow her up and remove her from this most uncomfortable situation. Kyle looked over at me and Phoebe, trying to figure out who we were, but didn't intervene. "Oh, well, I guess you don't want us to know. No problem. Do you have any messages for Jase? You know, in case we run into him later? I'd be glad to let him know we ran into you." I smiled my biggest smile and just stared at her.

"No, thank you," she tersely responded through gritted teeth surely wishing we would just walk away from her.

"Oh, okay then," Phoebe said matter-of-factly. "See you on the beach tomorrow!" She then grabbed my arm and pulled me away as I continued to stare Sarah down, conveying with my glare that I wasn't happy about her being here with Kyle without Jase's knowledge. As soon as we were out of sight, Phoebe turned to me and jumped up and down with excitement in her eyes. "That was so fun! Oh My God! Did you see her face? How great was that? We totally messed her up!" She continued jumping like she was on a pogo stick, clapping her hands and laughing.

"Yeah, yeah, it was great. Let's get back to Nick and get something to eat. I hate cheaters. I hope Jase breaks up with her," I mumbled as I pulled a very giddy Phoebe back over to the game Nick was still playing.

"Where have you guys been?" he asked us. "I'm running out of quarters here!"

"We just kicked some cheatin' butt!" Phoebe yelled, a bit too loudly, although it was funny. Nick turned and looked at her in surprise, questioning. "Oh, we'll tell you while we eat our sandwiches. Come on!" And she dragged us out of there and over to the meatball and zeppole stand down the other end of the boardwalk. Seemed we both worked up an appetite.

"You did what?" Nick asked again, feeling as if he hadn't heard correctly the first time.

Phoebe had no problem repeating and reliving the encounter. "We saw Sarah holding hands with some guy and so we asked her where Jase was!" She continued to be giddy with excitement over our confrontation with Sarah in the arcade. "She was so shocked! Like catching a kid with his hand in the cookie jar!" She picked up another zeppole, pulled off a piece and popped it into her mouth. "Mmmm. This is so good!"

"Are you going to tell Jase?" Nick asked, while chewing a mouthful of meatballs and dabbing his mouth with a napkin.

Phoebe and I answered simultaneously. "No!" "Yes!" We looked at each other, surprised by our obviously completely opposite opinions on this matter.

"We are not telling him. He may be hurt by it," I explained to Phoebe. Jase was so good to me that night at Matt's party, and we'd just had a great time swimming together, I didn't want to be the one to deliver any potentially hurtful news.

"Well, I'm telling him!" Phoebe proclaimed. "He's my brother, and she was out with another guy behind his back!" She was adamant that this was news she needed to share with him. We continued to talk it out with Nick weighing in, but never reached an agreement. Best to change the subject and let it sit for a while and then bring it up again later.

"Why don't you guys ride the carousel, and I'll take some pictures? I'm going to hang here and finish my zeppoles. Leave your stuff. Go on, Phoebe, have some romantic time with Nick." Nick almost spit his meatballs out at me across the table, giving me a look that confirmed that I just threw him under the bus, but with Phoebe's continued whining and coaxing he had no choice but to give in and go. The carousel was right next to the table where we sat, so I'd be able to get some good pictures without much effort on my part. Best of all, I could continue to shove zeppoles into my mouth to drown out my sorrows over missing Zack and seeing Jase get cheated on by Sarah.

I held my hand out for their phones. Nick placed his in my hand with a scowl to let me know that I'd be paying for this at some later time, before they both headed over to the ticket booth to get their tickets. Knowing I was once again spared the embarrassment of riding the carousel, I settled into my seat to relax for the next ten minutes. As I watched Nick and Phoebe standing in line talking, and laughing, I thought about how nicely their relationship had grown over the summer. Last year, we were all just friends hanging out and having fun. My mind replayed through all that had happened to the three of us this summer: Nick and Phoebe getting together, Nick saving a girl from drowning, Zack and I getting together, me getting saved by Jase, the whole mess at Matt's party, Zack confessing to me about how he felt about me, and now Sarah cheating on Jase. Man, summer was only half over. I chuckled to myself. *What the heck else can happen?*

The music from the carousel began to fill the air, bringing me out of my daydream and back to reality. I looked on as the horses and tigers flew by me on the carousel, watching the little kids wave to their parents as they made their way around and finally caught sight of Nick and Phoebe on two very nicely painted mares, one with a sparkly mane and tail and the other in rainbow colors. Leave it to Phoebe to find the two most girly horses on the ride! I picked up her phone and clicked through the settings to take a photo as they came around again. She caught my eye and posed with her arm around Nick's shoulder, making sure to ham it up a bit on my behalf. A few quick clicks with her phone, and then I set it aside to take a few with Nick's phone. As I reached for it, I noticed that he had received a text from Zack. I quickly tapped the message and read it.

Zack: Having a great time!

There was a photo attached. I tapped it to expand it into the full screen of the phone. As it appeared, I felt my stomach drop. I wasn't prepared for what was staring back at me.

Flee. Flee. It's all my brain could register. *Remove yourself from this. You shouldn't have looked. You shouldn't have looked.*

The phone slipped from my fingers and hit the table with a clunk. It startled me, and I felt my stomach twist. I had to remind myself to take a breath. *Breathe, now, just breathe.* I was frozen, my brain trying to comprehend what I saw.

It was Zack, and a girl. She was sitting on his lap, his arms around her waist. She had one hand in his hair, the other resting across his chest. He was smiling. She was smiling. Her lips were pressed to his cheek. A bottle of beer sat on the table next to him. His shirt was off. Hers was too. I felt like crying.

My phone continued to vibrate in my pocket as I ran down the boardwalk back to where we left the bikes. I weaved through the throngs of people, barely able to see where I was going as tears streamed down my face. *I'm not answering that. I don't care who it is.* For a moment I had to stop to figure out how far I'd run. I'd forgotten which street I had to find. I had gone about five blocks too far. I wasn't going to turn back. I didn't want to see anyone. I couldn't face anyone right now.

The sounds of the amusement pier began to fade as I made my way further away from the rides and the crowds. Nearing a beach entrance, I slipped through the gate and rushed as far as I could from the people and the lights. I wanted darkness and silence. I wanted no one. I wanted to be far away from the cheaters. I wanted to be alone. If I could, I would have run away from myself. I headed towards the water, running so fast that my flip flops flew off my feet. I kept going until the cool water touched my toes. I sunk to my knees. I put my face in my hands and cried.

What had happened to Zack? Just last week he told me how he'd changed. How meeting Nick had changed his life for the better. He told me how he respected me and how I was so different than those other girls he knew. I sobbed so heavily, I curled myself up in a ball, my head tucked into my knees, my arms wrapped around myself as I tried to find some comfort — there was none. The truth is that Zack had taken my heart and crushed it. I gave him my heart and he betrayed it.

What if I hadn't seen the message on Nick's phone? Would that have been better? I would be with Nick and Phoebe right now finishing up my zeppoles and not feeling this way. My stomach tightened and I felt the rise of bile in my throat. I was going to be sick. I turned my head just in time as vomit pushed through my mouth and onto the sand. My stomach continued to cramp and I gagged again, losing all of my dinner. I sank back down into a ball and cried some more.

Minutes passed, although it may have been hours. All I knew was that the waves continued to pound onto the shore and the lights of the pier still shined brightly. The crowds were all enjoying their night at the amusement pier and boardwalk. No one was sitting on the beach crying. No one was retching and sobbing. No one but me. I needed to get home. I needed this night to end, and along with it, all memories of Zack. My phone continued to vibrate in my pocket, but I still didn't take it out to look at it. I didn't want to talk to anyone. I pulled myself up, weak from crying and vomiting, but stumbled, using my arm to keep from falling into the wet sand. Once again pulling myself to my feet, I began to walk towards Cranberry Cove along the shoreline, further and further from the pier and back to the comfort of the Cove where life before Zack was easy and pure. I'd have to pick up my bike tomorrow, I couldn't think about that right now, I just needed to get home to my bed. I turned my mind to the task of propelling myself forward. *One foot in front of the other, just keep moving.*

The beach was empty. I walked one mile before reaching the familiar houses that looked out over the ocean and marked my entrance back to the Cove. The moon no longer sat over the water as it had earlier this evening. Instead, I could see only the black of night littered by a few porch lights that dotted the landscape; no doubt shining to welcome home those who were out enjoying themselves on this beautiful evening, no longer beautiful for me.

A low hum grew into a louder one as two lights approached from the beach in front of me. The beach patrol quad moved closer from the north, and with no place to hide, I stopped and waited in hopes that it wouldn't venture this far south in its rounds. As was my luck tonight, the quad rode up in front of me, illuminating my wretched self in all its glory, vomit-stained clothing and tear-stained cheeks.

"Casey! What are you doing out here alone? What happened to you?" In an instant, Pauley was at my side, hands on my shoulders, spinning me towards him to look at me in front of the quad's headlights, assessing what possibly could have happened to make me appear in such a state. Fortunately, it wasn't what he'd imagined, and only after I assured him it was all my own doing, did he finally release me and sit me in the passenger seat of the quad. He turned it off so we could talk quietly.

I spoke first. "Pauley, I'm okay. Just upset." I looked straight ahead, not being able to look him in the eyes. I was ashamed and felt like a fool, and was sure that it showed on my face as if a neon sign was attached to my forehead.

"Tell me what happened, Casey. Did someone . . . touch you? Hurt you?" His voice laced with urgency as he broached the delicate subject. I sensed his discomfort in asking what needed to be asked.

"No, Pauley, I told you, nothing like that. I'm just upset. That's all." I began to wring my hands together in my lap, releasing what little energy I had left, dropping my head now and focusing my eyes on the bracelet I wore, the dangling charms laying softly on my wrist.

"Where are you coming from? Why are you out here all alone?" His voice now a whisper, recognizing that it was comfort that would get me to speak to him, and not force. His police training was certainly being put to the test now.

I cleared my throat which was sore from the bile that had scorched it earlier. "From the pier. I was with Nick and Phoebe. We biked there tonight."

"If you biked there, why are you walking now?" I think he knew how difficult this conversation was for me because he moved his body closer and grasped my hand, pulled it into his lap, his other arm draped over my shoulder. This was the big brother role now emerging. He was concerned about me. No longer were we police-and-girl-on-the-beach. We were neighbors and good friends who cared about each other.

I couldn't answer him. The brave facade I'd been trying to put on for him collapsed and I fell into his shoulder. He quickly embraced me and pulled me closer, holding me and rocking me and whispering in my ear that everything would be fine. How could he know that? It certainly wasn't fine, nor would it ever be. Betrayal doesn't go away. It seeps into your heart and rips it open and brings pain — lots of pain — and my body ached from it. I tucked myself into his neck and threw my arms around it. I sobbed and apologized for my behavior. He just shushed me and tried to calm me. And I let him. For once since that text came through, I didn't want to be alone.

My phone vibrated in my back pocket. "Aren't you going to get that?" Pauley whispered in my ear as I continued to weep into his neck. "It could be someone who's worried about where you are. Maybe Phoebe, or Nick."

"I don't . . . want to talk to . . . anybody!" I cried, and without thinking dragged my runny nose across his shoulder.

"Let me look at it," he calmly said. "I just want to be sure it's not your mom worried about you. Okay, Casey? Will you let me do that? We don't want her to be worried about you." Before I could protest, he reached carefully around to pull the phone out of my back pants pocket, never once releasing his grip on me, letting me know he was there for me and wouldn't betray my trust, as someone else already had. He looked at the phone over my shoulder, and I heard him tapping the phone as he responded to someone, most likely telling them that I was safe.

"Please don't tell anyone where I am. I don't want to see anyone, Pauley." I sniffed as I spoke, burying my head into his shoulder and wiping my nose with the back of my hand. I pulled away slightly and looked at him. "Please," I begged, "I don't want to see anyone right now."

"I'm not telling anyone where you are. I just responded saying you are okay and you got home safely. That's all. It wasn't your mom. That's all I was concerned about." Pauley slid the phone back into my pants pocket and wrapped his arms around me again, rubbing my back. I was in no hurry to talk, and needed the down time to get my thoughts together. I wasn't sure how much of this I wanted to share with him. "Where are your shoes?" he asked, just noticing that I had carried nothing with me when he found me.

"I lost them on the beach by the pier when I left there." He rested his chin on my head and stayed silent, but somehow I knew that he'd eventually want me to talk. It was late, and he had rounds to do, and I needed to get home and out of these wet and vomit-splattered clothes. He finally pulled away and sat me up in my seat, taking my hands again in his. Our eyes met as I waited for the questions to come.

"I'm not going to ask you what happened. You'll tell me if you want to. My only concern was that someone . . . touched you or hurt you. You're telling me that didn't happen, and I respect that. Do you want to talk about it? I'm here if you do." Concern and sympathy looked me in the eyes, his voice sweet and non-judgmental. I felt my lip quiver as if tears would flow again, but the tears didn't come. I must have dried up the reservoir.

My voice, although weak and raspy from crying, did come. "Boys . . . boys are mean. They tell lies, and . . . a . . ." I closed my eyes and swallowed before continuing. "Zack lied to me, Pauley. And when I found out, I just ran. I needed to be alone. I left Nick and Phoebe on the carousel and took off. They're probably going crazy looking for me."

"Well, I responded to Nick's text so they know you are safe now. I probably spared you from them for tonight, but tomorrow you'll be on your own. I know how Phoebe is, and she'll want to see you in person." The soothing tone in which he spoke calmed me further.

"I know she will." I pulled my hands out from Pauley's grasp and settled back further into the quad's seat. "I didn't tell them I was leaving. I'm sorry about that now. I just didn't think." Looking straight ahead into the darkness, I could just make out the lights from the amusement pier in the distance. I marveled at how far I'd walked, thinking to myself how odd it was that I didn't remember how long it took me. My mind had been elsewhere, obviously. "I saw a picture on Nick's phone," I confessed in a whisper, as if hiding a forbidden secret. "He was with another girl, holding her. She was kissing him." I turned and looked at Pauley, his eyes watching me, hanging on every word as I spoke, "He told me I was different. That I meant something to him. I believed him. How . . . stupid of me." A chuckle escaped my lips. Not a happy one, but more of a realization and confirmation of how easily I had been fooled. Pauley's eyes looked kindly at me, and I could see the hurt behind them. The kind that comes with not being able to make someone you care about stop suffering.

"Sometimes boys don't think, Casey. They act on impulse. I'm sure if Zack could take back what he did, he would. He knows how special you are. I saw how hurt he was at that party when he thought you were in danger. He didn't want you hurt then, and I'm sure if he knew he hurt you now, he would be sorry for it." Pausing to think a moment, he continued. "Does Nick know you saw that picture? Because if he does, my bet is that Zack knows it now as well."

I took a second to think about what Pauley had just said. I hadn't thought of that. If Nick figured out that the picture is what upset me, I'm sure he texted Zack to tell him. I wondered if some of the texts that had come in as I walked down the beach were from Zack. I didn't want to look. I couldn't handle seeing his words right now.

"I need to get you home," Pauley said as he started up the quad. "I'll drive you, and tomorrow if you'd like, I can drive you to pick up your bike. Okay?" Even though I knew he was going to take me home anyway, he still asked me if it was okay. Pauley was my knight in shining armor tonight. I nodded and sat back in the seat, and he pulled the quad around and headed up to the dune opening and towards my house. I closed my eyes and felt the rumble of the quad as we made our way down the quiet streets of the Cove. Within a few minutes, he had pulled up to my house, which sat dark and quiet. I slipped out of the seat, thanked him again, relishing the smile and wink he returned before walked up the driveway and steps of my house, slipped in through the screen door and headed to bed.

"You don't feel warm," my mother said as she felt my forehead with the back of her hand for what seemed like the zillionth time. It was almost noon, and I still hadn't emerged from under my covers. "This isn't like you, Casey. Phoebe's been here twice to see you, and Nick stopped by, too. I kept telling them you were still sleeping."

I pulled the blanket back up over my shoulders as I turned in my bed onto my side, nestling into the pillow. "I just don't feel that well this morning, Mom. I'm going to go back to sleep for a while. I'll see Phoebe at work."

"Well, just send her a text and let her know, please. She's worried about you."

"I will, Mom. Thanks." I looked back over my shoulder at her as she grabbed my empty glass of orange juice and walked out, closing the door behind her. It took all the energy I could muster, which wasn't much considering what I'd been through last night, to pull myself up to a sitting position. Each movement was too tremendous an effort, as if the weight of an elephant was sitting on every part of my body. I dragged my legs around and let them fall over the side of the bed, using my arms to support me as my toes tickled at the throw rug beneath them. I lifted my eyes and stared blankly around my room at the pile of clothing I threw haphazardly around the floor as I stumbled into my bedroom last night after Pauley had brought me home. I looked for my flip flops briefly until I remembered how they flew off my feet as I ran from the boardwalk after seeing that text from Zack on Nick's phone. *Great. They were my favorite pair.*

I shook my head trying to remove the memories of last night from my brain, focusing instead on the task at hand. I needed to text Phoebe to let her know that I was up and alive and would see her at work later today. I knew she wouldn't accept that, and would be at my back door the minute she received my message. Careful not to look at any of the messages that came in last night, I just didn't have the mental capacity to deal with them at this point; I sent a new message to Phoebe.

Text between Casey and Phoebe:

Casey: Hey, I'm up. Not feeling great. Will see u at work.
Phoebe: K

I counted to ten. Then to twenty. Then I heard it. The knock at the door, and some words that I couldn't make out but sounded like two people exchanging pleasantries, and then my door creaked slowly open. Phoebe. I watched as she peeked around the door, as if asking permission to enter — I knew she wouldn't wait for me to respond. She just slipped in and then settled next to me on the bed. She waited a few seconds to see if I was going to talk, but I knew she wouldn't disappoint me. Once she started, it all spewed out.

"Casey, you doofus! We thought you were dead! Why did you just leave like that? And you didn't even answer your phone when we texted and called? What kind of a person are you? We were worried sick about you! You didn't even have the decency to let us know you were okay? We looked everywhere! And then we got to our bikes and yours was still there! How did you get home? Are you crazy?" Luckily, she needed to stop to take a breath, and the pause was finally the opening I needed.

"Are you through?" I asked, looking at her a bit sarcastically as if I could even answer one of those questions after she was throwing them at me in warp speed.

She took a deep breath and then threw her arms around me. "We were worried. Thank God you finally responded to Nick. You had us really worried!" I lifted my arms and returned her hug to let her know that I did appreciate their concern, and to apologize for leaving them to worry last night.

"It was Pauley who responded, not me, but I'm glad he did. I was in no shape or mood to even look at my phone last night. I still haven't looked at any of my messages yet." I nodded over to the phone that was now sitting on my nightstand. Phoebe reached over and grabbed it, thumbing through the messages. "If there's one there from Zack, I don't want to hear it." I made sure my voice left no doubt that I meant what I had just said to her.

"Nick texted him last night and told him what happened. He never intended for you to see that picture, Casey, and he feels really bad about it."

"Really *bad*? He feels . . . *bad*?" I stressed the word "bad" because I knew what I felt like last night, and there is no way he felt anything like I felt when I was puking my guts up on the beach. "Bad? Oh, poor Zack! He feels *bad*!" I made the sentence sound the most pathetic I could. "Well, I don't care what he feels! He can go to hell for all I care! Because that's where I was last night!" I threw myself back into my pillow and buried my head, but I didn't cry. I wouldn't give him the satisfaction of making me cry again over him. I had to be strong. There was no way I was going to let him ruin the rest of my summer. If anything, this entire ordeal set me free — free to do what I wanted, when I wanted, without having to think about what Zack was doing and who he was with. Now I could just go on and live my life, and put this behind me. That's what I needed to do now. Put this whole Zack thing behind me.

"Do you want to read his text?"

"No. Delete it for all I care. I'm done with him." I pulled myself off the bed, stood up, and then began to pluck the clothes from last night off my bedroom floor and toss them into the laundry basket. As I picked up my shirt, my bracelet fell onto the wood floor and made a tinkling sound. Both Phoebe and I looked at it as it picked up the light from the window, glistening and shiny against the honey colored wood. "My bracelet," I whispered, finally stating the obvious, but not moving to retrieve it. We both just looked at it. I looked at Phoebe. "I loved him." There, I finally said it out loud.

The next few days were difficult, to say the least, but thanks to Nick and Pauley retrieving my bike, and Phoebe keeping me busy at the beach and at work, I was able to finally get back into somewhat of a groove reminiscent of the old Casey, pre-Zack. It turned out that Phoebe had told Jase about Sarah and Kyle after she got home that night. Jase decided to request a different beach assignment in order to avoid seeing her up at the ocean. Unfortunately for me, that kept me from seeing him as well. But later that week a spell of bad weather had settled in over New Jersey, and that meant finding things to do that weren't beach related.

"I'm bored," whined Phoebe on the phone to me after two days of torrential rain. "Let's do something off the island. Let's go to the mall or something." I hated shopping, but by this time I was willing to do anything. Daytime TV in the summer was really, really bad.

"How are we going to get there?" I asked her, since we'd need someone to drive and pick us up since both my parents were working and unavailable for taxi duty.

"I'll ask Jase! He isn't working because the beach is closed, so he can take us. Hold on, he's in the other room." Hey, it sounded good to me, and he was probably as bored as we were. In about fifteen seconds, she was back on the phone. "He said yes! But he wants to do a movie, too. So be ready in an hour. He's probably going to call some of his friends as well. There's no way he would want to be seen with us alone." She laughed, and I did too at the prospect of Jase ever wanting to hang out with Nick, Phoebe and me. I just hoped that Blondie Sarah wasn't on his list of people that he'd be calling.

My rainy day beach attire didn't venture far from fair weather attire. Shorts and flip flops, but with a hoodie over my t-shirt, and I was ready to face whatever movie and mall stores Phoebe would have us suffering through today. A feather could have knocked me over when I ran to the car that had come to pick me up, and saw that Jase, Nick and Phoebe were the only people in it. "Just us?" I asked as I jumped in, taking down the hood from my head and looking into the back seat at a very cuddly couple.

"Yup, just us!" Jase replied, with a smirk. "You were expecting . . .?" He left that question hanging and waited for an answer. Gosh, he looked good sitting in the driver's seat of his old beat-up Camry. For a minute, I couldn't respond as he'd stolen the breath from my lungs.

"Oh, nobody, I guess. I just figured that others would, you know, be coming as well." My choppy response was the best I could have done with those eyes staring at me and how I ended up in the front seat with him was beyond me as well. I pulled on my seatbelt and clicked it into place, and with a smile in return to mine, he pulled away from my house.

General chatter flowed easily on the ride over the bridge that took us off the island and back into what other people would call civilization. There was definitely a boundary that one crossed when leaving Cranberry Cove and headed into the New Jersey mainland. You couldn't see it, other than it being the Barnegat Bay, but rather you felt it, and sensed it. It was more hectic, less special, less scenic, and the more you drove inland it became more . . . regular. Gone was that sense of fairy tale that you felt when you were in the Cove. Instead, more strip malls, car dealers, gas stations and houses with lawns were the norm. I watched out my passenger window as we passed the same old buildings, the same old stores, feeling a nostalgic appreciation for what treasure we all were able to enjoy on our island.

The movie theater was crowded, as to be expected on a rainy day in the summer. Jase left us off near the entrance and then parked the car while we found our place in the ticket line. The only movie we could agree on was an action movie about a spy in the secret service. A comedy would have been a bit more to my liking, but this would have to do. I was all prepared to buy my ticket, when someone jumped in front of me.

"Two for *The Forbidden Spy*, please." Jase pushed his way, politely, in front of me and before I could protest, he added quietly, "Don't even try it, Casey. This one's on me. I heard you had a rough week." Shocked, I wanted to crawl back under my hoodie and hide in the popcorn bin. What did Phoebe tell him? I turned to look behind me at her, catching her eye, but she obviously was too tied up in whatever Nick was telling her to know why I was glaring at her. Jase had already moved to the side with his two tickets in hand; looking smug and happy at just pulling a fast one on me. I really didn't want charity right now. I didn't want to be known as Casey-the-Loser. I wanted to go back to being just Casey.

"Jase, really, you didn't have to do that. Th-thank you, though," I muttered, moving over to stand out of the way of the rest of the masses of people trying to get their tickets. He looked at me and mouthed, "My pleasure," with a wink. *Well, if he was going to get the tickets, then I was going to get the popcorn and soda.* I grabbed Phoebe as she approached with Nick, and announced through gritted teeth, "Phoebe and I are going to the restroom. Be right back." I didn't give her a chance to protest, instead I grabbed her by the arm and tugged her in the direction of the restroom doors. She stumbled but regained her footing, waiting to protest until the door was safely shut behind us.

"What the heck, Casey? Why are you dragging me?"

"What did you tell him?" I was in her face, a sense of urgency in my voice, my eyes wide and full of fire.

"Tell who? What are you talking about?"

"Jase! He knows what happened with Zack!" My arms were flailing showing my disbelief. "What's up with that? How could you share that?" I took my hands and dragged them down my face, over my cheeks and my neck — my eyes looking up at the ceiling for who knows what — strength?

"It kind of came out when I told him about Sarah, and what you did for him. He was hurt by Sarah. And it kind of slipped that you were hurt by Zack. I don't know. It just came out in the story. I guess I just thought that misery loves company. I guess I wanted him to feel better. I'm sorry. I didn't mean to embarrass you or anything."

I leaned back against the sink counter and crossed my arms, hanging my head. The truth was out, and I knew I should just get used to it. It happened, there was no denying it, and Phoebe was right. Jase was hurt that night, too. Misery does love company, I guess. I looked up at her and smiled. "You're right. I'm sorry. It just caught me off guard. I forgot that he was going through his own hell that night as well."

"Can we get some popcorn now?" Phoebe smiled at me, eyebrows raised and sporting a pouty set of lips to show that I was depriving her of one of her favorite snacks of all time.

"Let's go," I said, nodding to the door. "And I'm buying!" We headed out and made our way back into the crowded theater lobby. "Wow! Where did all these people come from?"

"There they are! Over there!" Phoebe had a special radar when it came to Nick and she could somehow hone in on where he was at any given time, it seemed. I followed her pointed finger and caught sight of Jase and Nick, both holding large bags of popcorn, and one large soda each.

"Theater five," Jase said as we approached. "We got the snacks, so let's find some seats."

"I wanted to buy the popcorn, Jase, since you got the tickets," I protested.

"No way. My treat today, Casey," he replied, being a gentleman and stepping aside so I could move ahead of him as we made our way out of the lobby and over to the double doors of theater five. With his hands full, I at least was able to pull the doors open for him, a small consolation for his buying the tickets and the popcorn. The theater was darkened, and luckily the back row offered four seats, so we snuck in. I went first, Jase followed, followed by Nick, then Phoebe. By the time I noticed that Phoebe was on the far end away from me, the previews popped on the screen. There was no way I'd be able to move now. The realization that I would be sitting next to Jase through a two hour movie hit me like a brick. *Great. Awkward.*

Normally by now I'd be crunched over in Phoebe's ear as we watched and rated the previews. But I sat stiff as a board, not knowing where to put my hands or where to look, other than straight ahead at the screen. I looked to my left. Jase sat still next to me, the bag of popcorn on his lap and the large soda in the cup holder between our seats. He looked as uncomfortable as I did. He must have sensed me looking at him because he turned his head towards me and our eyes met. He looked unsure, but said in a quiet voice, "I'm glad Phoebe had the idea to get out and catch a movie today." A small smile graced his lips.

He looked so shy, and so sincere. He made me feel a bit better. "Me, too." I smiled back, and I felt sympathy for him and what he had gone through. I think we both knew what hurt and betrayal was, and found a bond of some sort in it. I was able to see my hurt reflected in his eyes, and it somehow relaxed me, and brought me comfort. Not in the fact that he was hurt, but that he knew what I was feeling. Today was a distraction that both of us needed, and we needed to embrace it for what it was. It was a way to put that hurt in our pasts and move forward. I was so ready to do it.

"May I have some popcorn?" I asked before diving into the bag.

"Of course!" he said as he moved it closer to me, holding it up to make it easier for me to grab a handful. "I hope you don't mind, I only grabbed one straw for the soda."

That caught me off guard. The sign. We both knew what one straw meant. "Ah, sure, no problem. I don't mind." I responded as my eyes dropped to my lap. *Whoa. One straw. How cool is this?* He took the straw out of his pocket and tapped it on his knee to free it from the paper wrapping, then stabbed it into the top of the soda lid, smiling and then settling back into his seat. Yes, he was proud of himself for moving on from Sarah. And I was relieved to be moving on from Zack. And as the previews ended and the lights dimmed even further, I sat back and let myself get lost in *"The Forbidden Spy,"* the bag of popcorn, a soda with one straw, and my favorite lifeguard.

Looks like you've saved me again, Jase.

Made in the USA
Middletown, DE
03 August 2015